Unsound

a Novel

by

Toby Neal

much aloha!

Toby Neal

Photo credit: Mike Neal © Nealstudios.net

Cover Design: © JULIE METZ LTD.

Book formatting: Mike Neal © Nealstudios.net

Ebook: ISBN: 978-0-9891489-4-8

Print: ISBN: 978-0-9891489-5-5

Unsound

A Novel

By Toby Neal

Like a city whose walls are broken down is a (wo)man

who lacks self control.

Proverbs 25:28

Chapter 1

*I*think I started getting really worried when I found the shoe.

I was done with my last client of the day and had opened the door to leave. There it lay on the jute mat leading into my office—a cream-colored leather heel splotched with mud, all by itself like a question mark. I picked it up and looked around as if its owner might jump out of the red gingers planted beside the building.

The little graveled parking lot was deserted. Not for the first time, I wondered if I should have chosen this remote location with its pretty little restored cottage set back from the University of Hawaii, Hilo campus. It had seemed a good decision—easy access and privacy for clients—but now I wished I'd taken the office space in downtown Hilo I'd been offered.

I set the shoe inside the door against the wall, aligned and pointed outward as if inviting its owner to reclaim it. The golden imitation-leather insole was printed with "Jessica Simpson" in curlicued girly writing. A few blades of grass were stuck to the sole, and mud had made a splash pattern on the sides and up the way-too-tall heel.

She had run in these. I'd stake my psychologist's license on it. I provide consultation and support services for law enforcement for the state of Hawaii, and maybe it was time to give one of my colleagues over there a call.

Next to the shoe was another find, a child's blue plastic ball. Beside that, a rhinestone-studded dog collar missing a tag. Each of these items, innocuous in themselves, had turned up on the office porch. Taken together, they were creeping me out. I couldn't help but remember the ordeal one of my clients, Lei Texeira, had gone through with a stalker. I hate stalkers, narcissistic bastards that they are. I really didn't want one of my own.

I locked the office door, looked around again, and walked

down the wooden steps. The yard guy needed to come. The gingers were getting a little leggy, and the grass, loving the wet Hilo weather, was trying to take over the gravel walkway. I beeped open my car—a cream-colored Mini Cooper special edition with real red leather seats. Its beautiful design, round retro dials and all, made me a little bit happy every time I got in.

And I needed every little bit of happy I could get these days.

I put my Bluetooth in my ear and called Captain Ohale over at South Hilo Station on his cell as I pulled the car out of my lot and onto the feeder road going past the University of Hawaii campus.

"Hey, Caprice. How ya doing?" Captain Bruce Ohale had a mellow voice, one of those that instinctively lowers the blood pressure—a very good thing in a station chief.

"Hey, Bruce. I'm good, busy. Been doing a lot of interisland trainings and consulting. You?"

"Nothing big. What's up? We haven't seen much of you lately."

I provided counseling to police department staff on the Big Island who either request it (seldom) or have mandated services (also seldom), but I also did training and consultation to all the islands, which kept me busy in addition to my private practice.

"Haven't had any cases with you folks. And that's a good thing. No, I'm calling to pick your brain about something." I got on the road, heading back into Hilo. I live on the outskirts of Hilo on the Hamakua side, and it's an easy twenty minute drive from the office. "I've been finding some objects outside my door while I'm in session working with people. Odd objects."

A long pause. I heard the whoosh of his breath as he exhaled a sigh. I pictured his big square hands pulling a yellow legal pad over, rubbing a ballpoint on the paper, the cell phone almost disappearing into his fleshy brown ear as he tilted his head against his shoulder to hold it in place. I could picture it because I'd seen him do it so often, those tiny steel magnifying glasses teetering on his wide nose.

"That's not good."

"I know. I'm having a Lei Texeira flashback." We had her in common, that extraordinary young officer who'd shaken up the station and continued to make headlines as she barreled after bad guys. Lei was one of my "success stories" and favorite clients, now a colleague as she requested me for consultation on her cases.

"No one's ever going to forget the campsite rapist case. Changed our community, broke the trust." He sighed again. I could picture him rubbing his eyes, the wobble of the glasses displaced to his forehead. "We're still recovering. So I hope like hell this is nothing like that. What kinds of objects are these?"

"Child's plastic ball. Rhinestone dog collar, no tag. Today a high-heeled shoe. Muddy."

"What color?"

"Cream, size eight, Jessica Simpson brand. The kind someone might wear to a wedding. No marks on it other than some grass and mud."

I navigated the downtown Hilo traffic as he wrote down the information. We have some big box stores on the edge of town, standard stop-and-go stuff until Hilo Bay, where things tend to get backed up this time of day. The town is utilitarian rather than pretty—Hilo had grown up around its natural bay as an area of transport and was the functional heart of the Big Island's commerce, not a big tourist attraction like Kona. Still, it's Hawaii, and the palm trees and lush ferns are everywhere.

"The shoe bothers me," I said.

"It all bothers me," Bruce said. "Any notes, anything threatening?"

"No, or I'd have called you sooner. Nobody around, and the funny thing is, I can usually hear people come up onto the porch of my office building. The items are outside, and I never hear anything."

"Are you taking precautions?"

"Just the usual." The usual is that I carry a handgun—a Glock 17—in my purse. I'm quite a good shot, actually. I also have some pretty intense pepper spray with an eight-foot trajectory, and I've been through the police academy's self-defense course.

"Well, how about putting in some sensor lights, maybe consider some video out there. Catch 'em in the act."

"Bruce. You know what I make, and this divorce . . ." My breath caught. He knew the basics, but that didn't mean I wanted to talk about it. "The divorce is kind of wiping me out. It's a whole new financial ball game."

"I'm sorry." Regret in his voice. "It's probably some harmless crazy you've worked with bringing you goodies, but just in case, I'm going to open a case for you under harassment-stalking. Is anyone coming to mind who this could be? Former clients, for instance?"

"No. I've been racking my brain." And I had. Truth was, I'd been so busy with the state job, my private practice had shriveled to a handful of clients, a motley mix who'd been with me for a long time and whom I trusted.

"Well, I'll open this and send a patrol by your office at least once a day for a while. If someone's watching it, maybe we'll scare them off. Really, consider more security for the building—and keep me posted."

"Sure that's all we can do?"

"Caprice, believe me. If there was more I could do right now, I'd be doing it." I described the items to him again slowly as he built my case file on the computer.

We said good-bye, and I hit the button on the Bluetooth, feeling a little better that he'd taken my concern seriously— but not better about the whole creepy situation. Well, worrying is a waste of a good imagination. Or so I tell my clients. Arguing with myself about how I was worrying occupied the rest of the drive home.

I pulled into the long driveway bordered by ornamen-

tal palms and way too much grass for one woman to keep
mowed. The driveway ended in a circular drive around a
flagpole, one of my ex-husband's designs—he'd named the
house Hidden Palms.

A flagpole and a house with a name—that should tell you
something about the pompous ass I'd married. It was a nice
house, though—natural lava-stone foundation, a contem-
porary design with one room flowing into the next, exotic
woods from Bali. Unfortunately, there was still a mortgage
on it, and by saying I'd wanted to stay, I'd been saddled
with an upside-down bugger of a payment. Richard had
found a way to hide all his money in his law practice, leaving me with my barely comfortable state job income and
private practice supplement. Ergo, lots of long hours working.

I slipped off my low Naturalizer sandals and put them on
the rack at the door, sliding my feet into fuzzy house slippers.

Hector trotted across the polished, echoing floor to greet
me in his loud Siamese, tail crooking from side to side, a
question mark changing direction. I tipped up his chin to
look into piercing ice-blue eyes in that seal-point face—

Hector always makes me a little happy too.

"Hi, buddy," I said.

"Meeerrrrrrow," he replied.

I wasn't going to drink tonight. Bettina had made me aware it was getting a little out of hand.

Bettina had been with us since Chris was a baby. She'd answered an ad for "part-time nanny and light housekeeping," and she'd been invaluable over the years to two working parents raising a son in a house that was too big for us to even pretend to maintain. Now, when I was alone, and frankly, couldn't afford her anymore, she still went by the store and bought me the basics and came out once a week to run the vacuum around and chase the cane spiders outside. Bettina didn't believe in killing anything, even cane spiders.

She'd decided I needed her, and I did.

She'd come yesterday and had waited until I got home. I was taken aback, as I got out of the car, to see a row of six large black plastic bags lining the wide steps up to the double front doors. They bulged with the odd but distinctive shapes of liquor bottles.

"Caprice." Bettina had her hands on her hips. A short, compact Filipina woman, her graying long hair pulled back in a braid, she put me on notice as she'd always been able to. "Here's your glass recycling."

"Hm. Seems like it's built up a lot in the last year," I said, echoing her posture, with a frown on my brow as if I had no idea how the bags of bottles had mysteriously multiplied.

"Caprice." She aimed her small dark brown eyes at me— they'd always reminded me of kalamata olives, such a dark brown I couldn't see the pupils—and they'd always been able to see into my soul. "This is the last three months. I am not stocking your wet bar anymore, and you can take these to the recycling center yourself."

"Okay," I'd said meekly, afraid she was going to tell me I had a drinking problem. Afraid if I heard the words, I'd have to do something about it. I wanted to apologize but couldn't figure out how to phrase it. She'd stomped back into the house to hang up the denim apron she wore when she cleaned. I trailed after her. "I've been going through a rough time, Bettina. It's hard to be alone out here, without anybody."

Bettina hung the apron on its special peg in the kitchen, turned back. "I know, and I'm sorry. But that's a lot of recycling."

It would never be her style to say anything more direct than that. She came over and hugged me. Her hair brushed my cheek and smelled like ginger. Her round, firm arms felt warm and strong, and I felt those easy tears that were never far from the surface prickle my eyes as I clung to her for a long moment. She set me back, gave my arms a squeeze to make me let go. "I gotta run. See you next week." She left.

I had to haul the bags of booze bottles out of sight to the back of the house, during which chore I decided to cut back. Tomorrow.

Well, now it was tomorrow and I was supposed to be cutting back. I felt that feeling, more like a hunger than a thirst, something I was always aware of nowadays. It flooded my mouth with saliva and a craving that seemed to originate in my very bones.

I wanted that *pau-hana* drink. I deserved it. I had a stalker to deal with, for God's sake, in addition to everything else. I sat down where I'd been kneeling on the shiny wood floor, petting Hector and trying to muster resistance.

I didn't quite know how things had gotten to this place, but I suspected it was a very long time ago, when I was fourteen, and half of me was lost in a bolt of grief that had never really been dealt with.

I'd lost everyone who mattered to me. I was alone.

One of a pair of shoes.

One of a pair of bookends.

One boob still dangling on the chest of a cancer victim.

My losses swamped me, a great wave that began in the hand touching the soft creamy fur of Hector's belly, rolled up my too-thin arm, and broke over my head with a roar.

I opened my mouth and a sob came out, followed by more. Ugly sobs that racked my body and stretched my face.

Hector was alarmed. He scrambled out from under my hand and trotted away, twitching his tail and commenting on my unseemly display.

Screw it. I'd quit drinking tomorrow.

I got up, my chest heaving with convulsive hiccups, and poured myself a glass of good chardonnay to start—Silver Creek. Today's events called for quality, and that first drink is the best one, the one for the good stuff. I went out onto the deck and sat in one of the Adirondack chairs. I looked out at the view. Hector followed and hopped up into my lap, starting his motorboat purr now that my noisy outburst was over, paws kneading.

Richard had chosen the site to make the most of a gulch at the back of our property, and the raised deck overlooked a deep ravine overgrown with tree ferns and tiny wild purple orchids. Keeping the *wiwi* strawberry guava and Christmasberry bushes trimmed took a lot of extra time for the yard guy—time I couldn't afford anymore.

If I sipped the wine slowly and closed my eyes, I could stroke Hector and imagine I heard Chris laughing, giggling, and running across the wide-open space, Richard chasing him like he used to do when we were a happy family. I couldn't bring those days back. But at least I could stay in the house where those memories happened. I'd had a life before Chris went to college and my husband left me for an acrobat from the Cirque du Soleil.

I still couldn't wrap my head around it. Of course Richard couldn't just diddle his secretary like a normal guy; he had to get with a twenty-two-year-old flying contortionist. Who can compete with that? It was a joke—but the joke was on me, enough to make even a psychologist indulge in the demon rum.

Speaking of, it was time for a refill. I got up and walked to the wet bar, my footsteps echoing in the empty, lonely, too big house.

I used to be a social drinker, just a couple of glasses of wine a week. Somewhere in the last year, the occasional glass of wine had segued into a daily necessity and now apparently not something I wanted to give up even in the face of embarrassing bags of bottles and my maid's disapproval.

I didn't stop thinking about sad things until the wine bottle was down to an inch.

By then I had the stereo blasting and was singing "Witchy Woman" and doing a little moonwalk. I had a few moves, back in the eighties. Hector refused to dance with me, even when I took hold of his paws. The music must have been up too loud for me to hear the car in the driveway, because next thing I knew, celestial chimes cut across the Eagles and I realized someone was at the door.

No one came out to my house. So I had to really think about what I was supposed to do next. I still had my clothes on, fortunately, but even I knew I was drunk as I listed toward the front door and applied an eye to the peephole.

Great.

Detective Kamani Freitas stood on my front step. I knew her from various situations and cases, and on another day she'd have been a welcome sight.

I cracked the door. "Whatever you're selling, I don't want any."

"Dr. Wilson." Kamani frowned, a slight scrunch of her smooth forehead. She has wonderful rich brown skin and could be anywhere from twenty to fifty, her lush black hula hair in a braid that brushed her waist. She put her hands on her curvy hips. "Can I come in?"

"Why? What did I do?"

"No, no. I'm sorry to bother you at home, but you weren't picking up your cell, and I was in the area. Captain Ohale told me you'd be home, so I thought I'd drop by."

"I smell a setup. He sent you to check on me." I opened one side of the double front doors, leaving her to follow as I headed back to the bar. "How do you feel about the Eagles? I think they're the best thing my generation produced. Drink?" I held up a couple of bottles. One was Patrón, the other some awful peppermint schnapps left over from last Christmas. I put it down and picked up the white wine, waggled what was left.

"I guess—I'm not technically on the clock anymore. Can you turn the music down?"

"Sure," I shouted. I set down the bottles and clapped my hands a couple of times and the volume went down. "Sorry. Didn't realize it was so loud. What would you like?"

"Some wine would be nice."

I switched to Maker's Mark and splashed the last of the Silver Creek into a long-stemmed glass for her. I followed the detective out onto the deck, where Hector was giving her the once-over. He decided she was okay, and wound around her ankles, commenting as he did so. Siamese are never short on comment.

"Beautiful place." She took the wine from me. I held on to the railing, realizing my feet were a very long way off. It was important to keep it together, though.

"Thanks. It's got a name. Hidden Palms." I sipped my drink. That whole thing about mixed drinks causing a hangover is an urban legend, in my experience. "My ex designed it."

"Well, he has good taste."

"Not anymore," I said, and knocked back the rest of the drink. "I think I better eat something. How about you?"

"Sure." She sat on one of the teak Adirondack chairs, Hector climbing aboard her crotch and purring. I walked back into the house, taking careful steps so that I got there without running into anything. I opened the fridge, one of those big silver side-by-sides we all got before the economic bad times made them outré.

"Got some cheese and crackers," I said, bringing a wedge of Gouda and a row of saltines on a cutting board back out onto the deck. Thank God Bettina hadn't stopped picking up a few food items for me during the week—I'd forget to shop.

"Thanks."

I set the snack on the low teak coffee table, sat next to her, and ate a cracker with cheese on it. Something in my stomach was a good idea—I had that floaty feeling, like nothing and no one really mattered. A good feeling, a feeling I liked—except when a detective was eyeballing me with that assessing look.

"I know what you're thinking," I said.

"You do?"

"You're feeling sorry for me. Poor Dr. Wilson, all alone after her divorce in this big empty house, drinking."

"I wasn't thinking that." Kamani sat up, helped herself to a cracker and cheese. "Should I be feeling sorry for you?"

Her big, brown, long-lashed Hawaiian eyes narrowed ever so slightly. "Because I know a lot of people who'd trade places with you in a heartbeat."

"Forget I said that." I ate another cracker. It was time to focus, and the food was helping drown out the siren song of another drink. "What do you need help with?"

"I wanted your opinion on a case. But I'm thinking I should have made an appointment." Kamani stood, brushed crumbs off her dark slacks, brushing all the way down to the floor so that Hector's hairs fell off too. "How about I meet you at your office tomorrow morning?"

"Let me check my book." I got up, made my careful way across the room to the entry, dug my beaded reading glasses out of my purse along with the little dog-eared date book that makes me feel more secure than saving anything in my phone. "I can do nine o'clock."

"Good." She came over, and to my surprise, embraced me. I felt the strength in her strong arms—she probably lifted or something. I needed to do something like that, but for now I just enjoyed her vitality, my second hug in three days. "I'll see you tomorrow."

"Okay." I shut the door behind her. I teetered my way

down the hall and took a shower. I had a good cry in the stall, where I wouldn't scare Hector. After all, I was the one feeling sorry for myself. I might as well do it up big.

I went to bed, wet hair and all—but not without drinking a quart of water and taking three preventive pills: two Advil and one Tylenol. One thing I knew how to do was head off a hangover.

Chapter 2

I unlocked my office at the South Hilo Police Station to meet with Kamani Freitas the next morning. I'd been able to unsnarl my hair by spraying it with detangler, dragging a comb through it with water, and blow-drying the whole thing. I'd spackled concealer onto the bags under my eyes and wore my reading glasses, choosing the pair that were partially shaded, an effect that was almost as good as wearing sunglasses indoors. In my usual outfit of blue polo shirt—supposedly the color of my eyes—orderly blond bob, and twill skirt, I was the epitome of respectable.

Maybe that would erase Freitas's view through the side door panel of me dancing alone to the Eagles with my cat and a bottle. Probably not, but it was worth a try.

I got behind the desk with my thermos of extra-strong black coffee and decided to stay there, keep the high ground. I'd brought my laptop, and I had a boatload of e-mail to pretend to be busy with when she got here. I glanced around the space. I hadn't done much with it in the last two years. Still had a couple of my son's high school paintings on the walls, my lounge chair, a leatherette sofa, and a coffee table with a Japanese sand garden on it, rake invitingly angled.

A penis, complete with testicles, was outlined in the sand garden.

Someone had pranked me. This wasn't the first time—my office door was locked, but everyone knew where the key was kept—in the key closet in the supply room.

I had to get rid of it before she arrived. I scuttled out from behind the desk and dragged the rake through the genitalia, had it all but gone, when I heard a knock. I saw Freitas's face looking curiously at me through the little glass window in the door.

I opened it for her, but stood back. "Detective Freitas, please, come in."

A full retreat to formal was in order, and I went back behind the desk to seal the deal. Kamani Freitas followed me over, set her giant Starbucks cup down on my desk, looked around, found a chair off the stack in the corner, and damn if she didn't carry it over and park it right next to me on the corner.

I unscrewed my thermos, poured some coffee into the shiny silver lid. "So. Glad we could reschedule. What is this regarding?"

"Sure you got enough coffee there?" Freitas's voice was dry. I tilted my head so my eyes were behind the tinting and sat back, doing my inscrutable psychologist face. I wasn't going to dignify that with an answer. "Well, I'm here about a case."

"I remember that much," I said, my tone equally dry. "What can I do for the Kona Police Department?"

"It's a new case. Someone's embezzling from the Big Island Land Trust, a big nonprofit that leaseholds and manages state lands. We have several candidates, and I wanted your take on who seems the most likely."

Freitas set a file folder on the desk.

"Detective Freitas. Kamani. This seems like the kind of

case best solved by a money trail. Why are you approaching me with this?" I sat back, crossed my legs at the knee, brushed imaginary lint off my skirt.

"True dat." She used a bit of pidgin. "We've uncovered three strong possibles. None of them have clear financial motive or anything solid tying them to the case so far. My chief has authorized me to get your opinion on these three to give us some more direction."

"I'm going to need fifteen hundred dollars, minimum, plus travel expenses," I said, thinking of putting in the security measures at my office with this windfall. "I charge five hundred dollars per evaluation, as you know."

Freitas gave me a long look. "I'm not asking for a full evaluation of each suspect."

I shrugged, making sure the blue tinting on my glasses covered my eyes. "Take it or leave it. I've got plenty of work." Truth was, I really needed this, but it wouldn't do to let her know that.

The detective sighed. "Okay, I'll tell the Chief you played hardball. Submit a bill." She stood up, tapped the folder. "I'll e-mail you everything else we have. When do you think you can get to this?"

"Next couple of days. I'll call you if I'm missing anything. Do you have any video on the suspects? Interview
transcripts, things like that?"

"We do have some surveillance footage. I'll send it on."

"Sounds good." I stood up and walked behind her to the
door.

"Do people often get into your office?" Freitas turned at
the doorway, a tiny wrinkle between arched brows.

"Oh, you saw that." I shook my head. "Some of the guys
are pretty immature. That's not the one that worries me."

"What do you mean? I'm still a little worried about *you*,
Dr. Wilson." Her dark brown eyes were wide with sincerity.

"Well, I'm going through a bit of a rough patch. Divorced
six months ago. Son left for college." I found myself tearing up behind the screen of my glasses. "It's just a lot to get
used to, but I'm handling it. Anyway, it's something else. I
told Captain Ohale about it already."

"Tell me too." She wouldn't be pried out of the doorway,
though I'd angled my body and held the door so she'd get
the message.

"I don't think it's anything serious, but we're keeping an
eye out and I'm going to use the money from this job to put

in some security measures at my office." I told her about the lineup of odd items outside my door.

"I don't like it," she said immediately. "That's a huge red flag, especially in your line of work. Please call and put that security system in today. I'll grease the wheels to get you a check as soon as possible. Keep my private number on your cell." She rattled it off.

I went back to the desk, fumbled around for a Post-it and a pen. I had to have her repeat the number. I kept my back to her so she wouldn't see me blinking back tears and how bad my hand was shaking as I wrote it down, the numbers almost illegible.

"Thanks," I said when I was pretty sure my voice was steady. I turned back around and there she was again, giving me a hug. Whispering in my ear.

"Hang in there. You'll get through this."

I felt her strength, smelled her smooth black hair with a hint of coconut shampoo, and then she was gone, waving from the door. "I'll get you the rest of that information. Call the security company today, please, so I don't worry about you."

"Okay," I said, through stiff lips, and she closed the door.

I was alone. I checked the clock—I had fifteen minutes before I had to leave for my private practice office and the first therapy appointment of the day.

I walked deliberately back to the door and locked it, checking that the window shade was down. I picked up the box of tissues, lay facedown on the couch, and let myself have a good cry into the cushion, padded by Kleenex.

The fact that a detective was concerned about my weird stalker had me scared too. The last thing I needed right now was a stalker complicating the shreds of life I had left. That grief I'd been suppressing and distracting rose up to swamp me again.

I craved a drink. The nerves in my body were reaching through my skin, questing through the air and reaching for it like vibrating, hungry antennae. Fortunately, I knew I had an emergency bottle of vodka locked in the file cabinet. After five minutes of full-blown howling, I sat up. Blew my nose, wiped my eyes. Went back behind the desk, unlocked the cabinet. I took out the bottle, unscrewed the top, and downed several big swallows of Grey Goose.

The relief was immediate. A bomb of warmth went off in my belly, roared down along my veins, and my twitching nerves settled like a cobra into a snake charmer's basket. I savored the feeling for a long moment and took another swig, resting the cool bottle against my forehead. I screwed the top back on, slid it into the drawer, locked it.

I got on the intercom to Captain Ohale. "Bruce, I need who you guys recommend for home and office security," I said when he picked up.

"So you decided to put in a system?" I heard him flipping through the fat Rolodex on his desk. "We hear good things about Hi-Alarm." He gave me the number. "They have good response time and sensitive systems, and I hear they're reasonable. I'm glad you're doing this. I was going to offer to front you something for it."

"That doesn't actually make me feel much better. Detective Freitas was concerned too. I have an alarm system at home, but do you think I should do something more?"

"Send your company out for a full system check and upgrade," he said. "It can't hurt. I want you to feel safe and secure. We need you to deal with our stress, not the other way around."

I chuckled, but I knew it sounded wobbly. "I'll feel better when all these things are in place. Thanks, Bruce."

I made the calls to the two alarm companies and ordered a new, full system with video recording for the office and an upgrade to the house system.

I stood and picked up my briefcase. Discovered that I felt better. Calm, clear, ready to face the day—and also ready to have another swig of Grey Goose. But I wouldn't. I wasn't an alcoholic. Just going through a rough patch.

On my lunch break, eating a yogurt and an apple at my desk, I scanned Freitas' file. She'd put together three stapled pages of background and history on each suspect. I'd need more, preferably some audio or video footage of their interviews or surveillance. Seeing the subjects really helped with my assessment process—the way they spoke, moved, their mannerisms and demeanor. The best scenario was always to do my own interviews, but there was no way to do that in a lot of these law-enforcement cases.

The first possible embezzler, Randy Pappas, was a mid-fifties vice president whose background was in marketing. Financial pressures presented themselves in the form of multiple children in college. I definitely knew how those pressures felt. I used my pen to underline "financial pressures."

That made me think of Richard and remember again that first breathless stab when he'd told me, "I'm leaving you."

I hadn't seen it coming. I'd known there was a continental drift going on, that middle-aged, less-than-thrilling rut, but we'd just finished Chris's senior year of high school. It had been a whirlwind of applications, deadlines, the trip to visit his chosen school—our alma mater, University of California, Santa Barbara. The graduation, the parties, the departure in a flurry of leis and excitement had finally ended, and I'd had a big case on Oahu. Richard had taken Chris to his dorm in California, gotten him settled, and flown out to Vegas, where his lover was performing at one of Cirque du Soleil's semi-fixed shows—a factoid he'd told me upon his return.

"I waited to tell you about this until Chris was settled at UCSB," Richard said. "I didn't want this to interfere with his transition to college."

"Wow," was all I remembered saying, as he went on to tell me he'd been seeing this woman for two years, and he'd filed papers to divorce me that morning. I could have the house if I took over the payments, and he was sure we'd both be better off in the end.

"You don't really love me anymore, either," he'd said.

And in spite of my paralysis, my overwhelming panic at such an upheaval, I realized that much was true. I was in the habit of thinking I loved him, and that had gone on for twenty years. Honestly, it had been good enough for me.

I wrenched my thoughts back to the present and grounded myself in my surroundings: papers on the desk before me, pen in my hand. My cool, cream-walled private office with its good impressionistic Hawaii landscapes surrounding me. The leather couch, my armchair, my desk, and interesting work to do. A bottle of water at my elbow and another appointment on the way. These things had not changed even though the ex, as I'd decided to call him now and forever, had changed everything else.

I just have to keep on keeping on. Another of my therapeutic sayings, right there to bite me on the ass.

Chapter 3

I stood up and hugged Alison. I'm short at five foot three inches, but she was even tinier. She'd always reminded me of a dandelion, a slim stem of body with a fluff of bleached-blond hair and nothing much to hold her down but the huge black purse she toted around—and used to shoplift.

Alison was a kleptomaniac, and she couldn't look sweeter or less likely to steal. She had big blue eyes and a Southern accent that pegged her as a Hawaii transplant, if the lacquered nails and jangly jewelry didn't give that away first. She'd stolen everything from diamond bracelets to a flatscreen TV, and she'd never been caught.

"Thanks, Dr. Wilson." We'd just finished our session. I'd been experimenting with hypnosis with her—kleptomania is an anxiety disorder, and it's resistant to treatment. None of our substitute behaviors seemed to beat the craving, obsession, and triumph cycle that she had going, setting off a cascade of feel-good brain chemicals as she "stuck it to the man" every time she stole. At least we'd identified her triggers—feeling frustrated or lonely.

I wished I could hypnotize away my own craving for booze. It wasn't a bad idea.

"Keep me posted. Please remember to track each day— triggers, how bad the cravings were, did you use your alternatives or give in, et cetera." I walked her to the door that led to the outer office, and Alison spotted the row of items on the inside of the exit door.

"Hey. That's my dog's collar," she said. "At least I think it is." She went over to the lineup of items, picked up the rhinestone-studded collar. "Yeah. The name tag came off a while ago. I thought it must have just fallen off somehow. How'd it get here?"

"I don't know. I found it outside." My heart lurched— what did this mean?

"Oh. I guess I had it in my purse and must have dropped it or something. Well, see you next week." She tucked the collar into that bottomless black bag and left with a little wave.

Well, good. One item had an explanation.

I followed her to the door and watched Alison walk to her car, a late-model BMW, and throw the big purse in. Pippi, her white toy poodle, had jumped up and had her paws on the dash. Alison reached into the bag and put the collar on the dog. She looked over and saw me watching, waved again. I waved back.

Mrs. Kunia drove up in her rusty blue Ford truck as Alison pulled out. Her husband, Frank, had built a wooden box on the back where he stored his tools, and a cluster of ti leaves dangled from the license plate for luck. A bumper sticker read, SLOW DOWN. THIS AIN'T THE MAINLAND.

Apelila Kunia got out, a tall, heavy woman in her late sixties, wearing a knee-length muumuu and rubber slippers. She made her deliberate way down the gravel path toward me, carrying a papaya the size of a bowling ball.

Mrs. Kunia's daughter had died a few years ago of a drug overdose, leaving her and her husband to raise the children—a girl, twelve, and a boy, ten. Henry, the ten-year-old, had been killed accidentally by Frank six months ago in a hunting accident involving his rifle.

"Hi, Mrs. Kunia," I said, holding the door open. "Come on in."

"Brought you something." She put the gigantic papaya into my hands. "You look like you need to eat."

I laughed. "Thank you! I probably do. It's beautiful." I shut the door behind us, followed her into the inner office, where she took her shoes off at the door, walked in, and sat on the couch. I set the papaya on my desk, where it stood upright, majestic as a sculpture. "Did you grow it yourself?"

"Farmers' market."

It was going to be one of those nonverbal days, then. I settled myself into my armchair with my clipboard on my lap and my pen at the ready. "Tell me how you're doing this week."

A silence stretched out.

Mrs. Kunia, the strong, sturdy Hawaiian woman with her cracked heels and hands rough from work, stared at the designs left by Alison in the little Japanese sand garden on the table. Finally, she reached forward to pull a handful of tissues out of the box beside the sand garden. She spread the tissues open over her palm, layering them over one another in a precise stack. When the stack was of a suitable thickness, she pressed the tissues to her face and let out a sob.

What a sob. It was deep, aching, a wrenching sound that brought tears to my eyes too, echoing as it did my own grief. I got out of the chair and sat beside her on the couch. I stroked Mrs. Kunia's back in little circles as she wept.

She saved it all for this office. She held it in and held it together as she must, for her husband who was eaten with guilt and for the twelve-year-old granddaughter, wild and angry as a cornered mongoose. But here, she let it all go.

I was there to witness her pain. Validate it. Support it.

It cost me to empathize with the pain of clients, to genuinely share it—and yet nothing less seemed to heal as powerfully; nothing less seemed to honor what they'd been through. Sometimes I wished I'd worked in the time of the old psychodynamic model—detached from the client behind the couch with a clipboard, a therapist who could do a crossword, say "uh-huh" and "interesting" and send a bill.

Mrs. Kunia cried for two-thirds of the session, and when she was done, she pulled out a new stack of tissues and wiped her face with them. Little strands of her thick silver hair had come loose from the topknot on her head and clung to her cheeks. I got up and opened the little fridge, took out a cold bottle of water and handed it to her. "Fluid replacement."

She gave a bark of laughter, unscrewed the lid, and drained half of it. "Thanks, Dr. Wilson."

"I didn't do anything. You're the one doing all the work." It's something I tell clients often. The work is theirs; I am just a facilitator, holding the emotional container for what needs to be processed, reflecting their own healing back to them so they can understand it better. That's why I don't worry about "engaging" clients, keeping them coming back. I'm here and solutions are here, but I won't ever work harder than my clients—because only they can do what needs to be done.

"Frank left."

"Oh no. Why?"

"He feels so bad. He says we're better off without him, especially with Maile still blaming him for the accident." Maile, the angry twelve-year-old who refused to come to my office. I let a long moment go on, wondering if she had anything more to add. She did. "I worry he's going to kill himself."

"Where did he go?"

"To a hunting shack he uses. It's on the mountain." The "mountain" was nearby Kilauea Volcano, where pig hunting is allowed in the park year-round with a license.

"Did he say anything about hurting himself?"

"No, but I know him. That's what he thinking. He took his guns."

"I agree he's at risk. Maybe he just wants to go somewhere and be sad; but a man alone and grieving in the wilderness with a gun is a recipe for suicide. Let's call it in."

"I no like. He'd be shame." Her voice thickened into pidgin. "He be so angry wit' me."

"His life may be at stake." We argued back and forth for a few minutes, and finally I said, "Remember when I told you what was confidential and what wasn't? This isn't. I have a duty to protect if I think there's a real danger of suicide or homicide."

Mrs. Kunia stood to her full five eleven. "I nevah tol' you fo' do that."

"I know. Blame me. Tell him the stupid *haole* doctor

wen' do 'em," I said with my best attempt at pidgin, and she shook her head and walked out, each footstep a stomp that shook the little old cottage.

But I knew she was grateful, and she'd be back. I just hoped we'd be in time to save Frank's life.

I looked up my ranger friend at Volcanoes National Park in my cell phone. Bridget was the sister of a client, and she took it seriously when I told her all I knew and that there was a very credible chance Frank Kunia was going to his hunting shack to commit suicide. "Where's the shack located?" Bridget asked.

I didn't know that. "Call Mrs. Kunia. She's reluctant to report this, so when you find him, if he's okay, could you guys make some excuse? Tell him you're checking his hunting license or something."

"Of course, Dr. Wilson. We'll get right on it. You know when someone's in danger. Thanks for calling."

I'd saved her sister's life. Sally's elliptic comments about ending it all in my office had culminated in a hanging attempt at home, which my call to Bridget had averted. Sally, my former client, was especially grateful. She was now married with a baby on the way. I gave Bridget Mrs. Kunia's number.

Mrs. Kunia was my last appointment of the day. I was rattled and behind on my notes. I liked to complete them after each client, but that hadn't been possible. I shoved down the longing for a drink that wound its way around my nerves.

I sat down at my desk and started my case notes, beginning with Alison's session, because doing what I needed to do had always calmed me. I still liked to hand write my notes, and I took out a fresh form and the gel pen I used for easy flow.

D: Met with A. 50 min. and reviewed progress on goal of reducing problem behavior to 1x wk. A. affect sad, worried. Did 20-min. round of hypnosis using suggestion that feelings of frustration or loneliness could be addressed by self-care steps like calling a friend, taking a shower, exercising. Assigned hw of tracking mood, level of craving using 1–5 scale, and number of times she was able to deflect an episode and/or indulged behavior.

A: A. has made progress managing behavior. Continues to come to sessions regularly but does hw only 2/3 days/wk. Anti-anxiety medication may assist more rapid progress.

P: Make referral to personal doctor or psychiatrist for

*trial of anti-anxiety medication. Discuss in next session.
Use motivational interviewing to explore ambivalence
around recovery demonstrated by sporadic engagement with
homework and follow-up activities. Continue trial of short
hypnosis during sessions as A. says she thinks it's helping.
Monitor if actual incidents decreasing to verify.*

Caprice Wilson, PhD

I'd gone to the DAP (Data, Assessment, Plan) note-taking format some time ago as it captured all the information I needed in a less-cumbersome format than the SOAP notes I'd learned in college. I also liked to keep clients' confidentiality protected as much as I could even in my notes, since the insurance companies, ever vigilant of fraud, made us sign contracts to turn them in whenever asked for—a fact the public wouldn't find palatable at all.

It wasn't in Alison's best interest for anyone to know that her "problem behavior" was stealing, and my priority was my clients and their recovery.

Which always brought me up against one of the moral dilemmas of life as a psychologist. Most of my practice was with law enforcement, and here I was, basically hiding a thief. Fortunately, my ethical standards were clear. Unless the problem was causing harm to another, I had an obligation to protect confidentiality—and while it could be argued that kleptomania hurt the economy and retailers in particular, there was no direct physical harm to another as covered in Tarasoff and suicide or abuse reporting laws.

Perhaps Alison would be helped by a little jail time—but I doubted it. It was my job to help her on her journey to beat the problem herself. It still staggered me to picture Alison, with her tiny arms and feathery hair, lugging a giant flat-screen out of J. C. Penney, unchallenged.

And it was still my job to protect her, particularly from someone who might have approached her because I was her therapist—but hopefully I was overreacting, and she'd just dropped the collar somehow.

Alison had drawn a series of hearts in the sand garden with the little rake. Her design had survived the tears of Mrs. Kunia. We'd talked about her learning to love herself and that stealing wasn't congruent with that. She'd drawn those hearts as she talked. Her relationships with men were a staggering series of disasters—she tended to like them with fast cars and gambling problems. I felt my affection for her rise up—she really was like a dandelion, fragile-looking but tough.

Maybe there was a third scenario. Alison was a compul-
sive liar when she was stealing. Maybe she'd spotted the
collar, wanted it, and told me a lie. It was entirely within the
scope of her behaviors and actually wouldn't surprise me.

The security system was going to be put in tomorrow;
there was nothing more to be done right now. I'd just have
to live with the uncertainty.

I took out a fresh sheet and began Mrs. Kunia's progress
note:

*D: Mrs. K. arrived with gift of fruit (culturally correct
gesture on her part.) Affect flat, few verbalizations. Cried
for 25 minutes. Disclosed fears of suicide for husband.
Disagreed with this practitioner's decision to notify Park
Service and left upset. Followed through with notifying Park
Service personnel Bridget Fukuda of concerns at 4:35 p.m.;
referred personnel to Mrs. Kunia's cell number for location
of Frank Kunia's reported destination.*

*A: Mrs. Kunia still experiences feelings of deep grief
frequently, and fears for her husband triggered this bout of
extreme crying. Though ambivalent about reporting, and
outwardly angry with my decision, Mrs. Kunia knew what*

she was doing when she told me and the kind of action I

would take. She was able to relieve herself of the responsi-

bility of making the necessary calls, which could set her up

for relational problems with husband later. She has difficulty

with disclosure and self-reflection, skills that would help her

navigate the losses she has endured.

  P: Follow up with Park Service tomorrow to see if they

located Frank Kunia. Continue to work with Mrs. K. on

developing a broader range of self-reflection and communi-

cation skills.

Constance Wilson, PhD

I sat up abruptly, looking at the signature. *Constance*

Wilson.

My dead identical twin sister was trying to take me over.

It was one of my very old fears, part of what had led to

keeping her firmly locked away in my mind. I reached into

my desk and took out the white-out tape, carefully erasing

her name. Constance was definitely making her presence

known—that bright presence, so charismatic that even

before I knew what it meant to be a twin, I'd known she was

the original and I, the copy.

I wished I'd been able to grieve for her normally. Maybe

she wouldn't haunt me so much now, in my current pain.

Caprice Wilson, PhD, I wrote, over the white-out tape, pressing hard.

Constance's sudden death, hit by a car at age fourteen, had left me frozen with unspeakable loss. Numb. Cauterized as if halved by a lightning bolt. I'd been unable to cry or speak for weeks. When I did finally start talking, I couldn't say her name or speak of her. I never did cry. I'd been hearing what sounded like her voice in my head lately.

You've got grief issues, Caprice, and that's making it harder to deal with the divorce, that voice said now.

"Damn you, Constance. Why'd you have to go and die?" I whispered aloud.

I filed the case notes, locked the cabinet, and turned off the lights. When I went to the door, I peeked out through the window. No one was parked in the parking lot; no one was on the porch. I put my hand into my bag, unzipped the interior pouch where I kept my Glock, and curled my hand around the cool pebbled grip.

I unlocked the dead bolt, stepped outside, scanning like my law-enforcement friends had taught me, and saw the sun striking pink and gold off high cumulus clouds behind

Kilauea Volcano in the distance. To the right of me, the clustered buildings of University of Hawaii were lit by the orange flame of blossoms on the African tulip trees.

Clumps of towering torch ginger, at least six feet high and until now something I'd treasured, blocked my view off the little porch. Someone could be behind them and I wouldn't be able to see them—but otherwise, there was nothing out there but the lush overlong grass, empty little parking lot, and my Mini Cooper waiting for me, a dollop of whipped cream steel.

I finally let myself look at the mat—and there was another object there.

Chapter 4

y heart fluttered as I scanned the area. The white mug sitting there had not been there earlier, and it was doubtful Mrs. Kunia would have stepped over it on her way out and not said something. I bent, keeping my eyes moving, and picked it up, then backed into the office foyer and flipped the bolt to lock the door.

I turned the mug in my hands. Cheap china with the words WORLD'S GREATEST GRANDMA emblazoned on the side. This was Mrs. Kunia's most prized possession, a gift from her dead grandson. She'd brought it in one day to show me. She would never just leave it on my mat, never!

I felt sick with a creeping horror, a nauseating feeling

like the ripples of an unseen wind blowing across my skin, raising gooseflesh. Someone was stalking me by stalking my clients. Someone had taken that little poodle's collar off and brought it here, left it on my doorstep like a cat leaving a mouse. Someone had taken the mug out of Mrs. Kunia's unlocked truck and left it here when she'd gone, probably while I was making my phone calls.

But maybe she'd left it for me. Some sort of statement, or gift, or symbol of moving on. I could be overreacting. It was maddening not to know what was going on. I walked back into my office and called Mrs. Kunia from my office phone.

The call went to voice mail, and I said, "Mrs. Kunia, I know you're upset with me and not taking my calls, especially if the rangers have contacted you. But this is important. Did you leave your mug on my doorstep for some reason? The one Henry gave you? Please, call me back on my cell phone and let me know if you did. It's very important."

I left my cell phone number and hung up. I did a couple of relaxation breaths.

There was no way to know right now. I'd just have to keep vigilant as if the threat was real but remain calm while I collected all the facts. Both of those items could have been placed on my porch by their owners, and the other two were unknown.

I carried the mug back into the entry room and set it beside the muddy high-heeled shoe.

I checked the window again, scanned again, my hand on the Glock. No one was there, nothing on the mat. I took my hand off the weapon, stepped outside, and locked the door.

I was probably getting paranoid with all the stress. Calling Bruce again seemed overkill when I wasn't 100 percent sure of the origin of the new item. He was doing all he could already—maybe I just wanted to hear his big, calm voice again.

What I needed was a good chat with a friend—and I would have called someone if I had any friends to call. Driving home, I wondered how that had happened. It seemed to have been a slow erosion. My friends from college were scattered all over the United States and we were still in touch, but not enough for me to call one up and vent about my divorce and a "maybe" stalker. Over the years, friends we'd had as young parents had moved, and we'd moved to Hawaii and left everyone in California. We'd had country club friends when I was with the ex, people he thought were worth networking with for his firm. I'd played my role with them, but mostly I'd been consumed with work and being a mom to Chris for the last few years—and it had left me isolated.

I did have my mentor, Judy Dennis, a retired psychology professor—but she'd been asking uncomfortable questions about my drinking lately and made no secret of her own membership in AA. Maybe it was time to tell her it was getting hard to cut back. Still, I just wasn't up to trying to explain the layers of what I was going through and how drinking helped me cope. It sounded wrong even to me.

Fortunately, the home security guy had been able to come out that day; he'd texted me the new code for the door and put in motion sensors in a formation around the exterior of the house and an auto timer to enable the system if I forgot to arm it.

This meant that once we were inside and the house was armed, Hector was going to have to stay in for the night. He wasn't going to like it.

I drove down the long driveway to the house. Automatic lights had come on with the timer, and one pointed at the limp American flag dangling from the pole. Once again I was irritated, seeing it. I'd always hated the way going up that driveway made me feel—pretentious, plastic. A California transplant, not someone embedded in Hawaii like I'd become. This was in the jungle, in Hilo, not a country club—but the ex had preserved that feeling in the layout of a house I wasn't sure I loved anymore.

I didn't have to have that damn flag out there if I didn't want to. There was a lot in the house I didn't really like and never had. Tonight might be a good night for purging. The hunger for a drink hit me hard as I unlocked the door, along with a wave of anger.

Anger at the ex, for turning my life upside down without permission.

Anger at Constance, for leaving me to muddle on without her.

Anger at the stalker or whoever the hell he was.

Anger at what I was becoming—not myself. A shaky, drinking shadow.

I'd always been a shadow—Constance's shadow. Richard's shadow. I toed out of my shoes and set my purse and phone on the side table.

Hector greeted me loudly.

"Hey, buddy." I fed him before I strode to the wet bar—
I still have some self-control. But after the second shot of
Patrón gave me my sea legs back, and the third and fourth
made me start to feel clear again, I decided I'd do a little
bonfire.

Richard had already cleaned his shit out of the closets,
but he'd left a lot of knickknacks behind, the kinds of things
that would have reminded the Acrobat that he had another
life before her—things like family photos, golf trophies,
cuff links, and a gold watch I'd given him for our anniversary.

I took a big shopping bag out of the kitchen and began
scooping his stuff into it: the aforementioned gifts, his
family's ancestral Bible (maybe God would strike me with
a lightning bolt), photographs framed in silver of us as a
family. I filled the shopping bag with anything of his I could
find and a lot of mine too—those stupid stiletto heels he'd
wanted me to wear when we had "kinky" sex; the golf shirts
and glove I'd worn to please him on the course, golf being a
game I found boring and pointless; scarves and purses that
he'd alternated giving me on birthday and Christmas the last
ten years.

There were twenty of those. I'd never used them, and he hadn't noticed.

I thought I'd been happily married—but come to think of it, had I been? I didn't remember being really happy since those early years, both of us building careers, sharing a passion for Chris and our identity as a family. The smart, accomplished, and good-looking Wilson family.

Coming home from work in the evenings, we'd sit on the deck of our little starter home in Hilo to compare stories. Richard had always said the law was full of psychopaths, and I'd agreed. Come to think of it, things hadn't really started their slow drift until Richard became obsessed with work and building Hidden Palms. We'd had a few good years here in the beginning, I thought, dumping a rack of his less-favored ties into the shopping bag—but I didn't think I'd paused long enough to really wonder until it was too late and he was pole dancing with the Acrobat.

The jewelry he'd given me and the anniversary watch I'd take to the pawnshop. I hadn't totally lost my marbles.

I carried the bottle of Patrón, the lighter fluid, and the barbeque lighter outside and set them on the steps in the darkening evening. A light wind tossed my hair as I hauled my loot out into the turnaround in front. The fronds of the palm trees clattered like applause. Hector followed me and sat on the top step watching, his tail twitching back and forth, as I made a big pile at the base of the flagpole.

I stopped periodically to slug Patrón. It went down smooth and kept me fueled.

"It's therapeutically important to make a ceremony of endings and beginnings, Hector," I said, lowering the American flag, draping it over the pile of items. "I'm going to make a ceremony here. This is the ending of my marriage and of putting up with anything I don't like in my home and my life. This is the beginning of the new, liberated me."

I realized I was wearing one of those polo shirts, a lot like a golf shirt, and it didn't feel right anymore. I tore off the shirt, unzipped my sensible twill skirt. "I don't think this is really my style. I don't know what my style is, but this is not it." I tucked the clothes under the flag. I was warm from the booze and enthusiasm and didn't even feel the cool night air pucker up my nipples.

"Hector, you're the witness to my declaration of independence!" I squirted lighter fluid over the pile and held the barbeque lighter out to touch it.

The flames burst up in a fireball, scorching my hand, and I realized I was burning both the American flag and a Bible. My heart pounded with terror, and I shut my eyes and waited for the lightning bolt.

None came.

I was standing close enough to the fire that it warmed me in my underwear, and I sat down on the grass and finished the bottle while watching the flames. But even drinking couldn't stifle my sense of loss this time.

My identical twin, Constance. The one that sparkled bright, the one with the flair. She was gone, and I was the pitiful broken-down divorcée that was left. It just wasn't right, or fair. It felt like a crippling weight—I was living for both of us, and what a failure at that I'd become.

Constance. What a misnomer for that gossamer spirit, that whirligig of impulsivity. She'd been a natural per-former, and even though we looked the same with our slim build, blue eyes, and blond hair, it was always Constance friends called for, Constance who sang in the talent show, Constance who won awards for everything from art projects to dance numbers.

I'd never resented it. Her successes lit me, standing in her shadow, and that was more than enough. I enjoyed that she did everything well—somehow that meant I didn't have to, that I already knew I could.

That was only one of the mysteries of being a twin.

Chris had asked for a brother or sister many times over the years. Richard wouldn't have been opposed, but I was adamant. "No, Chris, you're better off as an only child," I'd said.

"Why, Mom?"

I'd never been able to explain that the pain of the loss of a sibling was so much worse than never having had one at all.

I must have passed out, because rain was falling on me. Big, fat, cold raindrops. Hilo rain is powerful when it gets going. Rain was hitting me in the eyes, collecting in all my nooks and exposed crannies.

I sat up, smelling something horrible—something like melted plastic. I hit my head, opened my eyes. The timer lights had turned off, but the dim solar ones around the walkway were on, glowing like green mushrooms, and I saw that what I'd hit my head on was the flagpole. It had fallen over me where I lay on my back on the ground, and somehow it had missed pulverizing me.

I remembered the flagpole was made of resinous plastic. Perhaps making a bonfire at the base hadn't been the best idea.

I got up, or rather rolled over onto my hands and knees. I felt sick, and I had the whirlies. I dry heaved but there was nothing there. The beginning of the mother of all hangovers was gathering behind my eyes.

I couldn't even think about it now. I crawled up the steps and tried to open the door.

It was locked. Which was part of the new upgrade—if I didn't lock the house, it locked automatically at ten p.m. And it armed itself. We'd changed the code today.

Where was my phone, with the text with the new code on it?

Of course. Inside the locked house, in my purse, with my keys.

But no matter. I'd probably tripped the alarm when I moved into the sensor's range, and help would be on the way in the form of local PD, whom Bruce had put on alert about my residence. I'd be there to greet them. In my underwear, in the rain, in front of a burned-down flagpole.

I stood up very carefully. There had to be something I could do. I teetered back down the steps and around the side of the house to the gardening shed. The rain seemed to ping off me like evil BB pellets, cold and painful. Mercifully, the shed wasn't locked, and I stepped inside, into its warmish, dry, total darkness.

I spread my hands and stumbled forward, feeling the air in swooping motions, trying to remember with my battered brain where things were.

I connected with something tall, fabric-covered, that gave under my hand. I recoiled. Immediately my mind supplied the ex's corpse, strangled and stuffed in my gardening shed as a "present" to me from my stalker.

I made myself reach my hand out, feel the object again, patting it.

Ah. Not the ex's corpse, but a burlap bag of mulch. That was wishful thinking. I kept feeling forward. I knew what I was looking for—a blue plastic tarp I used to pile weeds on when I got the urge to tidy something. The gardening shed had been the yard guy's terrain for a while now; no telling where it was.

I barked my toe on something metal—further investigation told me it was the mower, which I knew was parked at the back of the shed. So that meant on my left was the table where we stored various implements. Maybe the tarp was there, folded up.

The rain drummed relentlessly on the steel roof, an overwhelming timpani of sound. Musty smells of mulch and manure formed a substance in my nostrils and throat, activating my gag reflex again.

Suicide flickered across my brain, a viable solution, as my hand fell on the sickle. I could cut my wrists the right way—straight up to my elbows from my wrists—lie down in here, and it would probably be over by the time the cops found me. It almost seemed like a better idea than being caught in here in my underwear, still drunk, with the remains of my angry divorcée bonfire on my front steps.

My left hand curled around the sickle, lifting it, and just then my right hand touched the square plastic softness that had to be the tarp.

I took my hand off the sickle, shook out the tarp, hoping there were no centipedes, roaches, or cane spiders in its folds, and wrapped it around myself.

Somehow, dimly even through the rain and the cushioning darkness of the shed, I could hear the wail of sirens.

They were here.

I lifted the tarp over my head, tightened it around me like a crinkly plastic burka, and walked back into the rain to face the cops.

Chapter 5

*B*ruce handed me a cup of coffee. His warm chocolate-brown eyes were crinkled with worry even though he smiled. "Quite the drama, Caprice. Didn't know you had it in you."

"I'm full of surprises." I took the cup. He'd made it black, the way I liked. I closed my eyes as I sipped. Closing them was an exquisite relief since they throbbed like hot marbles.

"I can see that. So much for the security upgrade. You're going to laugh about this someday."

"I hope so. It's hard to imagine that. I've never been so embarrassed in my life." I kept my eyes closed to avoid looking at him, but I could feel the heat of tears well-ing, bursting out from under my swollen lids. I was in my voluminous terry-cloth robe after a hot shower. The alarm company had given the responding officers the code, and they'd deactivated my new alarm while grilling me over my semi-nakedness and the fire reeking in my turnaround. It was hard for them to believe I'd done it all myself, and I'd had to call Bruce to get them to leave—but now he wouldn't leave either.

"Doesn't your wife wonder where you are?" I asked.

"Divorced," he said. I opened my eyes. Things were a little blurry without my glasses, but I could see the compassion in them, the kindness. He'd always been a good friend, and I'd never felt any hint of anything toward him but collegial friendship. I'd assumed he was happily married—there were pictures around his office of his grandkids in soccer outfits.

"I didn't know that. Well, then, maybe you know a little bit of what I'm going through—a rough patch. Entirely normal for me to be a little distraught." I looked around. "I need some Advil. Like really a lot of Advil."

"I think you're drinking too much."

I felt defensiveness rise up. "You're in my home in the

middle of the night. Yes, I got blasted and burned my ex's shit and got locked out of my house. It's embarrassing. But it's never impacted my work, and I'll get through this."

"I think you need some help to get through this." He reached over and took the mug out of my hand, set it on the table. His big brown hands chafed my small cold ones a long minute. "Do you have anyone you can call? I don't want you alone out here."

"I don't want to be alone out here. And no, if I did, I would have called them." I felt the tears return. Weak, self-pitying tears. "I thought about dying tonight. It scared me."

"I'm not surprised you had those thoughts." His mellow, calming bass voice worked its charm, and I felt like telling him everything, all of it. He didn't get to be chief without some interviewing skills. "It's okay. It's a hard thing you're going through."

"It's not okay for someone in my position to be in this state. I think I need to take some time off." The words popped out of my mouth, and I immediately wanted to take them back. What would I do without my work? I'd have nothing to do all day but drink and burn stuff and cry. Suicidal thoughts circled like black crows.

"I don't think that's a good idea without you going somewhere. Perhaps a spa, or a rehab place? You need some TLC." His hands were still massaging mine.

I felt something happening, a dim tingle of something warm, as if those hands were rubbing two sticks together to light a fire. I suddenly knew that this man, my colleague for the last seven years, someone I'd never been attracted to before, could make me feel very good indeed.

I yanked my hands away. "Rehab. Geez."

"I'm just saying you need support. You shouldn't be alone in this big house."

"I agree with you there." I stood up, and it was a mistake. I felt my knees buckling, and I sat back down on the couch. "Could I get that Advil now?"

He stood up. I looked up at him from the new vantage point of two divorced people, alone and lonely in a big house at night. He was tall, with the solid burly bulk of a Hawaiian man in the middle of his life, his buzz-cut black hair threaded with gray. Probably prediabetic, needed to lose some weight—and yet all I could think about was how warm that bulk would make me feel.

My mind provided a contrasting picture of the ex, with

his careful workouts and Pilates and golf. Every inch of his body was cared for and tweezed. He took his own blood pressure and weighed his food. His icy blue eyes and ash-blond hair matched mine. We were like Aryan bookends, and I'd never questioned that our fit was perfect.

That made me sad on some profound level.

Bruce returned with the bottle of Advil. I poured four into my palm, threw them back with a coffee chaser. I'd finally remembered what had gotten me so upset in the first place.

"I'm still worried about the stalker thing. Something new happened." I told him about Alison and the dog collar and Mrs. Kunia's mug. "So I don't know. Mrs. Kunia hasn't called—I just checked my phone. And Alison's not credible. I mean, I love her, but she's got compulsions, and she could have had a slip right in front of me."

He just sat down across from me in the good leather arm-chair the ex used to watch TV in and gazed at me.

"I'll sleep out here on the couch," he said. "And I want you to go on leave as of tomorrow and go somewhere safe and get help. If you don't do it yourself, I'll document this and get you fired."

I recoiled as if slapped. "You would never know about

this if you weren't my friend. I can't believe you'd kick me when I'm down."

"I'd know about this. I had to send two officers out to your house to respond to an alarm for a colleague I care about who may have a threatening client. I get out here to find you could have burned down your house or been crushed by a falling flagpole—in your underwear, suicidal and drunk. This is not a rough patch. This is an intervention."

His raised voice brought the hairs up on my arms, and his brown eyes were hard as pebbles in an icy stream. This was the police chief I knew and respected, whom I'd watched deal with every kind of disorderly behavior from officers and perpetrators alike. He was no pushover.

"Okay. Damn." My mind was too fuzzy to decide what to do, but I could see the necessity of getting away for a few days. "I'll go somewhere, take some days off. Now can I go to bed?"

"You need help, a program or something. At least a spa." He flipped his hand. "One of those celebrity beauty things or something. You could have massages every day and a personal chef."

My mind was too spongy to respond with anything coherent. "Okay."

I'd figure a way out of this tomorrow.

"Can I get it in writing?"

I looked up, and that crinkle of humor was back in his eyes. "Ha-ha. I'll show you where the sheets and blankets are."

I wasn't even embarrassed when he had to help me back to bed. I'd just been through an intervention, and there was nothing to hide anymore. Apparently things were bad, and I really did need help. There was a measure of relief in admitting it.

Morning wasn't kind and neither was Hector, disliking being shut up with me. His yowling at the door got me up and staggering across the overlarge room to open it and let him out into the house, where he could exit via his kitty door. Down the hall, I glimpsed the upright shape of Bruce sitting on the couch. He turned and grinned at the sight of me.

"Morning, sunshine."

I bit back a curse word and shut the door.

So it all had been real. There was no God. If there was, this would have all just been a bad dream. I'd burned the ex's family Bible and the American flag, been rained on and almost clobbered by a flagpole, and worst of all, I'd agreed to go to rehab.

In the shower again, hoping that would make some sort of difference to the worst hangover I remembered in years, I thought strategy. My strategy was . . . well, I couldn't think of one, but I had to do something to get out of town and dodge a possible stalker—and live down the gossip at the station from my divorcée bonfire—and maybe even admit I had a drinking problem.

I seemed to remember doing that last night. I must have been really drunk.

I got out and made the mistake of glimpsing myself in the mirror. I hurried past that and into the bedroom, stopped in front of the closet.

I wanted to dress in my style. Only I didn't know what that was. I knew only that the row of polo shirts and chinos of various types just wasn't it anymore. That look was left over from my life with the ex.

I pulled on pair of yoga pants and a long shimmery, silky

blue tee. I felt comfortable and easy in it, not like I'd just come off the country club golf course—something I'd never do again if I could help it.

I brushed my wet hair as I headed down the hall. "Got coffee?" I asked Bruce. He held up his mug in reply. "Good."

I went into the kitchen, struck by how big and excessive every single copper-bottomed pan I never used was. This *Architectural Digest* kitchen wasn't me, either. I got out my favorite mug, a delicately hand-thrown pottery one with a raku glaze Chris had made in a ceramics class and given me for Christmas.

Yes. This was still me.

It was a weird new landscape ahead, and I didn't have anything to navigate with but an internal compass—my intuition—saying *yes* and *no*. The difference was, I was finally listening.

I filled the mug with black coffee and headed back into the living room. "Did Hector go out?"

"Hear the blessed silence?" Bruce asked.

"Yeah, he has a way of making his needs known." I sat down on the leather armchair this time.

Bruce looked rumpled, his slacks creased. He'd taken off the short-sleeved button-down he'd had on when he arrived but had kept on a thin white undershirt. His thick, muscled forearms were propped on his elbows as he two-finger typed onto a laptop. I spotted a couple of tribal tattoos on the insides of his arms, and I found that intriguing, wishing I could see what they were—and where they went.

"I've found three possible rehabs for you. One's on Maui, two on Oahu."

"Oh." That was a cold shower on my momentary interest. I took a big swig of coffee, promptly burned my tongue. My eyes still felt gummy in spite of the shower, and my head throbbed rhythmically with the beat of my heart. "I'm fine. I can stop drinking anytime. I just haven't wanted to. After last night's debacle, I want to. No need for all that."

"I seem to remember that we had a deal." Bruce looked up. He had a big square head and his neck was nearly as wide. The brown of his skin contrasted with the silver of his buzz-cut hair. He narrowed hard cop eyes at me. "You go, or you get fired."

I opened and shut my mouth a couple of times. Heat flooded me in an ugly flush—I knew what it looked like when that happened, great crimson blotches mottling my fair skin, beginning on my chest and rising up my neck into my cheeks like the mercury on a thermometer.

"Fuck you," I whispered. "I don't deserve this."

"Yeah, you don't. But it happened anyway—your husband left you, your son went to college, and you've developed an alcohol problem. I care about you, Caprice—or I wouldn't be here sweet-talking you into doing the right thing."

"Sweet-talking? Shit!" I exclaimed. I wished I could pace around, maybe throw something, but I felt limp and kind of like a Chihuahua barking at a bullmastiff. I buried my nose in my coffee cup, trying to think of something smart and psychological to say. "I think you're projecting your mother issues onto me."

He just snorted, turned the laptop for me to see. "That all you've got? Pick one. You're going."

"No. Let me do it on my own."

"You're too far gone. I've got years of experience with this. I know what I'm talking about."

"I see. You do have mother issues. Was she an alcoholic?" Old psychologist trick—deflect attention from self with something angrifying. Sure enough, his big hands tightened on the laptop like he wanted to throw it at me.

"I'm referring to my experience as a police officer dealing with hundreds of alcoholics through my years on the job," he said, every word measured out and pinched off. "You're too far gone to do it alone. Pick one."

I was trapped. But maybe I could wriggle out of it if I went far enough away. I hate anything institutional, always have. I'd been on too many boards at those rehab and treatment places—there's no mystique. I just couldn't see myself believing the propaganda at the meetings and filling out little worksheets about my triggers.

"Okay. Maui. Always wanted to see Haleakala," I said. "You know that means House of the Sun."

He went back to typing, then working his phone, and before I quite knew what was happening, I was in the bedroom packing a bag with the four or five clothing items I could find in the closet that felt like the "real me," and I was getting into a taxi.

"Wait!" I stopped, the taxi door open. "Hector!"

"I'll take care of him," Bruce growled. "I'll come out to this crazy-ass *haole* house and take care of him. I'll keep an eye out for your stalker while I'm at it."

"Oh my God. Thank you." I trotted back and hugged him. I'd never done that before. His big arms closed over me, and I felt warm, safe, and tiny. I leaned my cheek on his chest, and the sound of his heart was big and slow and had a swish to it.

I never wanted to leave the sound of it.

"You have a heart murmur," I said. "You should come. Do a spa treatment or something, take off some weight."

"Sassy, you," he said, and turned me, pushing me toward the taxi. "Call me and tell me how it's going in a couple of days."

In the taxi, I finally looked down at the paper he'd ripped off and stuffed in my purse with the particulars of the rehab place. Called Aloha House, it was a mixed-gender treatment facility in the "gracious natural environment of Upcountry Maui" and boasted "medically assisted detox, counseling, classes, and meetings."

Screw that.

I could do this. I had another plan in mind entirely, an idea that had popped into my mind the minute I'd said

"Maui." Richard and I had always talked about a trip to a very special destination there, but we'd never actually made the time for it.

I turned away from a last sight of Bruce with Hector beside him and the melted flagpole fallen over into the driveway like a lost erection. Fortunately, I'd been able to squirrel a bottle of Grey Goose into my carry-on, and a little hair of the dog began to take the bite of the hangover away. After a few medicinal sips of vodka, I called Chris, needing to hear his voice.

"Hey, Mom." He sounded right next to me, not thousands of miles away at University of California, Santa Barbara. I immediately pictured him on the campus, my old alma mater and that of the ex. Where we'd met, in fact.

"Hey, hon." I injected my voice with mom-cheer. "How's it going?"

"Fine." He'd taken a reasonable first-year load, and now in the second semester, seemed to be finding his stride. "I'm on the way to practice." He'd joined the water polo team, his comfort in the water a gift from growing up in Hawaii.

"Oh. Okay. Well, I just wanted to let you know I'm going to Maui for a week or so."

"Oh yeah? You never go anywhere for fun."

I cleared my throat. "I might start. Anyway, this is a little—medical thing. I'm getting something done."

"Boob job?"

"Chris!" I exclaimed.

He laughed. "Hey, why not, Mom? You're still young. Why should Dad have all the fun?"

Why indeed.

His careless words burned like a whiplash. I wanted to hang up on him, but I didn't. I breathed through it.

"Mom, you okay?" He seemed to be really tuning in for the first time. "I'm sorry. That came out wrong. I just don't like to think of you alone . . . you know. Working. Feeling sad."

"Well, that's why I'm taking some time, taking care of myself," I said carefully, wiping tears off my cheeks with little flicks of my fingers. "You're right. I deserve some fun too, so I'm going to have some. I'll call you when I get back."

"Love you, Mom," Chris said. "Dad is an asshole."

"Yes, yes, he is," I said. It was the first time I'd openly agreed with anything like that statement.

Chris had said things like that before, had refused to see his dad at Christmas or meet the Acrobat. In return, the ex had quit paying his half of the college tuition, landing it back on me. I was fighting that one with my lawyer. Ever mindful of putting Chris in the middle, like a good little psychologist, I'd refused to hear Chris's anger or encourage it. I'd told him to "work it out" with his father.

Well, the ex *was* an asshole, and cutting Chris off only proved it in a whole new way. I was done being Dr. Feelgood over the whole thing.

"Hey. Can you come visit me at spring break?"

This was February. Spring break was next month. I crossed my fingers that I'd have the money. "Of course. If you want me to. Or I could bring you home."

"I'd rather stay in Santa Barbara. Show you some of my favorite hangout places."

Santa Barbara. Smells of eucalyptus. Glassy green ocean, squeaky white beaches, date palms and red tile roofs, hikes along the cliffs. Oh, I had favorite hangout places there too.

"I'd love that, honey." I felt a new closeness to my boy—a child who'd always tried to please his father and come up short. A child who was, in personality, a little introverted, artistic, but with a quick mind tempered by a sense of humor and bone-deep athleticism. He was born running, swimming, and climbing.

He'd love what I had in mind. Maybe I'd take him someday—someday when I was strong and sober. Whoever it turned out I really was, after the divorce dust settled.

"Love you, Mom. I'll look forward to seeing you then."

"Love you too. Talk soon." I punched the Off button.

For the first time I felt like I really wanted to stop drinking. Chris's heart would break if he knew what had happened to me last night, how close I'd come to being crushed by that flagpole or cutting my wrists with a sickle, like a genuine loony tune.

Like one of my clients, in a dark night of the soul.

Somehow I'd fallen into my own very deep crisis without realizing how bottomed out I was. It was time to take back my life, beginning now. I'd show Bruce. I'd show myself. But I'd let myself have one more day of drinking. The withdrawals were going to be bad when they started.

Just one more day of drinking.

"Hilo Airport, Aunty," said the young local driver, pulling up at the curb. I looked at the familiar low building and felt a hit of optimism buoy my energy.

"Thanks." I tipped him extra for calling me "aunty," a respectful title for older women in Hawaii. On the half-hour flight, I managed to put away three Bloody Marys by ordering one drink but three of the little liquor bottles.

I picked up a Dollar rental when I got to Maui and found my way to a Sports Authority in the main town of Kahului, where the airport was located. I parked in the busy lot and made my way into the football-field sized superstore. Just the racks of hiking boots made me dizzy, and I remembered something I'd loved about Richard—he was a careful researcher of any purchase.

He'd read *Consumer Reports* and shop out of season to get the best prices. He'd always taken care of things like this for me, had even bought me a new tennis racket just the week before he left me—as always, it had been just right for my grip and ability level. He'd always taken care of me in this way, and I missed him all over again. I was sorely out of practice doing my own shopping, not sure what I needed, and I felt paralyzed by too many choices. I sat down abruptly on the padded bench used for trying on hiking boots.

I realized I'd been trying really hard to focus on what

an ass he'd been and not all the many ways we'd cared for each other in twenty years of marriage. I might not have been passionately in love, but I'd loved him. The father of my child. My partner in life, my male counterpart.

Shit. Now I had to figure out my own goddamn shopping. I blinked hard. I was done crying. I waved a sturdy young saleswoman over.

"I'm hiking Haleakala Crater. I need pretty much everything."

She beamed. "Let me take care of you."

I bought everything she recommended from the skin out. Now was not the time to skimp on the charge card; this was rehab, and rehab cost a lot.

Laden with plastic-wrapped hiking gear, I spotted a Liquor Barn across the parking lot. I bought a bottle of vodka and ate a solid lunch at the food court. Then I got into my bright red Ford Fiesta rental and headed for the top of the world.

Chapter 6

*M*aui is the second largest of the Hawaiian islands, though it's still dwarfed by my home island, nearby big sister Hawaii. Maui's got some great features, and Haleakala, the volcano that dominates one side of its figure-eight shape, is one of them. Haleakala, unlike the Big Island's volcanoes, which are still active, has been dormant for two hundred years. The crater on top of the volcano is a world-class hiking area accessible only via foot or horseback.

This was the trip Richard and I had talked about for years, and now I was going alone and on a mission. It felt bittersweet, inevitable somehow, as I drove the narrow, winding, breathlessly scenic road higher and higher through rolling pastures and stands of eucalyptus.

The air is thin ten thousand feet up, at the top of Haleakala. Standing at the residential-looking check-in station of
Haleakala National Park, I had my first glimmer of doubt.
This trek might not be a good idea, but I'd been able to re-
serve two cabins, the first one for four days and the second
for three, on the floor of the crater. A week should be long
enough to get through the worst of the withdrawals.

The ranger, a fit-looking older Japanese woman with the
kind of sun-struck skin that reminded me of the neck of a
turtle, took a copy of my driver's license.

"Emergency contact?" she asked. I gave Chris's number,
realizing in that moment that no one in the world knew
where I was.

"Do you have any health conditions?"

"No," I said stoutly, thinking of the nausea, chills, shakes,
and hallucinations that might be ahead. Well, maybe it
wouldn't be that bad. After all, I hadn't been an alcoholic
for long—no more than a year, tops. "I'm in pretty good
shape."

She did a long, slow blink, but didn't outwardly disagree
as she finished the paperwork. I looked down at myself. I

was still in the yoga pants and shimmery blue tee from the night before, with a pair of sandals on my feet. I knew I'd lost weight in the last few months and hadn't been doing yoga or playing tennis, as was my habit—but a lifetime of fitness would surely carry me the mere six miles downhill to the first cabin. Mercifully, I'd left my hiking gear, still covered with plastic and tags, in the rental—I could well imagine her scorn on seeing it.

"You'll need to carry out everything you take in, including toilet paper," she said. "We have a 'Leave No Footprint' video for you to watch."

"Okay."

"You sure you want to do this?" she asked suddenly. "This is a long time out there you have planned. It would be better to go with someone."

I felt a twinge in the region of my heart that reminded me of the thousand unfulfilled dreams of my married life that I was burying on this trip. "If I had someone to go with, I'd be with someone. Sometimes you just need to go do it."

She must have seen something in my eyes because she finally smiled and gave a little nod. "Good for you. Well, there are frequent hikers through the crater, so if you get in trouble, just wave someone down. We also have ranger patrols that go through every so often to check everything's working in the cabins. We'll keep an eye out for you. You won't have any phone reception in the crater, so make any calls you need to before. Remember to boil your water; there's plenty of it, but it's untreated."

That and the Footprint video and I was ready.

Back at the car, I stripped all the tags and packaging off of the backpack and the pair of hiking boots I'd bought. I slathered some sunscreen on my face and arms and put on the billed hat with the detachable sunshield that covered my neck. I packed the backpack with all the food, my last bottle of vodka for a week, and two liters of water, which I figured was enough to get me to that first cabin six miles down the ominously named Sliding Sands trail.

Because I'd heard the Sliding Sands was difficult to ascend, I'd decided to park the car at the other end, the Halemau`u exit of the trail. This meant I had to go park it where I wanted to exit, then hitchhike to the summit with my pack—the first leg of my journey.

Driving to the parking lot at the Halemau`u trailhead, I kept craning my neck at the incredible views. I was now well above the clouds, above the island spread below like a throw net over a lush reef. Maui was as enchanted-looking in shades of green and turquoise as that first glimpse of Peter Pan's Neverland when the clouds parted.

As I was getting out of the vehicle, a sharp breeze, thin and blue as skimmed milk, cut through my clothing. I dug out the parka I'd had enough presence of mind to pack that long-ago morning. I took a hit off my water bottle, ignoring the craving for a hit of vodka as well, and hoisted the backpack.

It was heavy. Very heavy. Probably thirty-five or forty pounds of heavy that I was ill prepared to carry a hundred yards, let alone six miles through sand. Oh well. Let the hell begin. I beeped the rental locked and began the trudge to the main road.

My new boots were technically the right size, but there was a telltale tightness in the toe box. Hopefully thinner socks, which I had, would take care of it. At the main road, I stuck my thumb out and was surprised by the feeling of vulnerability and rejection that swept over me as each vehicle passed me by. God, to be doing this at my age and stage of life—humiliating.

Hitchhiking was not an endeavor for the faint of heart or those with any other choices. I reminded myself I was not faint of heart, and I didn't have any other choices (unless I wanted to hike back up Sliding Sands, which I'd heard equated with Dante's eighth ring.)

A few more cars passed, and then a couple in a rental SUV pulled over. I got in the backseat, out of breath with the effort of trotting to catch up with the car and carrying the backpack from hell. "Thanks," I panted. "I'm going to the summit to hike the crater."

"We can tell," said the driver, a beefy man in a red shirt that proclaimed he'd SURVIVED THE ROAD TO HANA. "Seems like a big backpack for a little lady like you."

"I'm going in for a week, so I had to bring a lot of supplies," I said. "Where are you folks from?" Old psychologist trick—deflect interest from self by asking more questions.

"We're from Canada," the wife said.

I got their entire social history and family dynamics and was mentally composing my evaluation by the time they pulled into the main summit parking lot. "Good luck with your hike!" the wife said.

I saved my breath by giving them a smile and a wave and

set the pack down at the trailhead while I trotted to the rest-
rooms—one last trip to the bathroom, sitting on a real toilet,
was to be savored.

Washing up, I let myself finally take a good look in the
mirror, a long steel expanse screwed to the wall behind the
sinks.

My skin was sallow. My eyes were sunken in pits of
shadow, and I'd never known I had so much craggy cheek-
bone. My blond hair was tangled and transparent, like the
tentacles on an anemone. My clothes hung like my shoulders were a hanger.

I looked like a meth addict on a bender. Worse even than
I'd feared and avoided seeing. Well, this was bottom. It
could only get better from here.

I splashed water on my cheeks, made sure I'd scraped the
last of the mascara out from under my eyes. I washed my
hands one last time, feeling a certain ceremonial, supersti-
tious wonder as I did so, a naive hopefulness like a girl at
her first communion.

This was the journey of a thousand miles that began with
a single step—one of my favorite therapeutic sayings. I was
going to hike Haleakala Crater all by myself, surrounded

by gorgeous nature, with no booze anywhere for miles and miles, and I was going to get sober.

At the trailhead, I lifted the backpack. It was so heavy it took all my strength to haul it up onto a rock. I squatted down and stuck my arms into the straps, hoisted the pack onto my back, and tightened the belt. It wasn't until it was on and I'd jiggled and settled and adjusted the straps as best I could (as if somehow that would make it lighter) that I walked to the lip of Haleakala Crater and looked over the edge.

Chapter 7

*T*he crater swooped out in a vast, deep blue arc of space and depth of gravity before me. Volcanic gravel, sand, and dirt in the colors of melted Crayolas poured in a frozen waterfall of rock down to, and beyond, the trail. The path of soft, deep gray sand was unobstructed by anything so gratuitous as vegetation; other than the metallic-green pincushions of silverswords punctuating the cinder, there wasn't a growing thing for miles.

I was slightly heartened to see a dust cloud halfway down the switchbacked ribbon to the bottom, which marked the movement of other hikers, and that gave me the courage to start down.

The air was so clear that distance was distorted. A cinder cone—a miniature volcano within a volcano—looked near enough to spit on just below me, yet I knew from the park map I'd picked up that it was at least four miles away.

I couldn't look at the views without stumbling, and that meant stopping. It didn't take long to realize that the more I stopped, the harder it was to start again. My boots sank into the sand at least two inches with each step.

I set a goal to make it to an outcrop below, one that looked like it had a rock or two to put the pack down on, probably a mile ahead. *I'll put the backpack down*, I told myself and have a nice big drink of water. *And some vodka*, a sibilant voice in my mind whispered. Booze had a voice too, and it was weighing in. *Just a little sip. Everything will feel so much better.*

Because things already weren't feeling good. The stiff new leather of the boots rubbed my ankles, and I hadn't remembered to change into thinner socks so the dread toe jam continued. I was winded already, sucking air like an asthmatic. I felt perspiration springing up along my hairline. I knew I smelled like the alcohol working its way out of my pores and sweat: a reek with a musty, sharp edge to it like old people and chopping garlic.

I bet the Acrobat never smelled like this. I bet she'd bounce down the trail with a forty-pound pack at a jog, and if she sweated at all, it would smell like vanilla and phero-mones. I couldn't even hate her. She was twenty-two, barely older than Chris. Just a child. She couldn't possibly know what she'd done to me—and her "prize" was getting Rich-ard, for God's sake.

I imagined him asking her to check if the electroly-sis he'd had done on his back hair was still working, like he'd done with me. He was so lovably vain. Or at least I'd thought it lovable. Just goes to show the power of rational-ization. But maybe he'd pretend for her, as if he didn't hang on to every vestige of youth with all ten manicured nails.

Richard was a good man in a lot of ways. He was a hard worker, did a lot of *pro bono* for the Hawaiian community. He'd had a way of really listening to people, his handsome head cocked, his clear blue eyes intent, that made people feel like they were the most important person in the world. He'd had a big laugh, and he'd known his vanity was silly. We'd even had our own inside jokes about it, and I'd checked him over regularly for moles and stray hairs, like a good baboon wife.

He's a son of a bitch. Hope he gets a disease and his dick falls off, Constance said. She sounded really angry on my behalf. Angrier than I was, come to think of it.

I stumbled over a rock on the trail, and the lurch forward pitched me off balance. I overcompensated, listing to the right—dangerously close to the long, unbroken sweep of harsh cinder that didn't stop until the bottom of the crater, at least a mile straight down.

I landed on my hands and knees, deeply grateful for the rock biting into my palms, the sharp-edged sand grinding into my kneecaps. I rolled onto my butt and took the pack off. It promptly flopped over, dust obscuring the new fabric in a whoosh. This was a good spot for a pit stop rather than the outcrop, I decided. I made the mistake of looking back up the trail.

It didn't look like I'd come a hundred yards.

Distance is deceiving here, Constance said. *You can do this. Besides, if you quit, you have to walk back up that, hitchhike your ass back down to the car, and then go to Aloha House with its "medically supervised detox and counseling."*

Ugh. This hike couldn't be as bad as the alternative. By the time Bruce found out I'd ditched Aloha House, I'd have kicked the booze and figured out what to do with the rest of my life.

I got out the water bottle, took a long pull. Got out the vodka bottle. Took a smaller pull. I had only one bottle to ease me through detox, and it would be better to wean myself off than end up totally cold turkey with more hard physical hiking to do.

I dug into the backpack and found the tightly rolled packet of thinner socks. Loosening the laces of my boots. I was dismayed to see red marks on my legs from the chafing of the tops of the boots and that my toes were already reddened, pulsing with pain as circulation reentered them.

There was nothing to do but put the lighter socks over my sore toes, work the boots back on. This time I tucked the abused yoga pants down into the boots and laced them over the lightweight fabric.

A gust of wind kissed my cheek with spitting grit. It would be bad if I didn't make it to the cabin tonight—it was going to be very cold in not too long. Getting up and getting the backpack on was a multistage process, one so difficult it made me decide I didn't get to stop again until I had reached the bottom of the crater.

Always a student of the mind, my own included, a part of me observed the free-floating anxiety I experienced, the mulling over my cases, the possible stalker, the hundreds of tiny unfinished bits of business I'd left uncompleted on the Big Island, including Detective Freitas's case—which I'd at least thrown into the backpack in its folder.

There is a Zen that occurs after that first hour or so when the decision has been made not to stop anymore. Gradually the swirling of random thoughts settled, like those tiny white snowflakes in a plastic globe, and all that was left was the physical discomfort. My breath tore through my lungs with a sound like ripping cloth, and I concentrated on slowing it down, trying not to hyperventilate as my lungs looked for oxygen that simply wasn't there.

My feet were better in the thin socks, but the downhill angle continued to pinch my toes into the boots. I felt my lower back begin a deep ache that had to do with being unused to bearing burdens of any kind, let alone forty-pound ones.

And I could smell myself. That was the worst thing of all.

I'd always disliked body odor, my own especially.

I reached the bottom of the crater with what had to be the slowest time ever in the history of hiking and felt the sharp afternoon sun wicking that rancid sweat up into the dry air, surrounding me like a really bad Pier 1 fragrance dispenser. I headed for the only shade around, a large clump of *mamane* bushes with a churned-up tie-out rail in front—apparently some people got to ride into the crater in saddle-sore comfort.

Under the bush, I took the pack off. I felt dizzy with exhaustion. I got out my beef jerky and chewed a piece, drinking water, and that helped a little.

The desert floor of the crater spread before me, rugged grasses beginning the process of taming raw lava into soil. Sunbaked hardy ferns and the tough little native shrubs called *pukiawe* were making inroads, and silverswords continued to punctuate the expanse, explosions of symmetrical grace notes. Over the whole spare, vividly colored landscape, the extravagant blue sky was the only excess.

Chortling and bobbing, several grouse approached me, dancing back and forth as they begged. They were bright and round, unfamiliarly marked. I was sure they weren't native, and they were panhandling like pros.

"You don't want my beef jerky," I said. The birds were not discouraged. One trotted up and pecked my bootlace.

A little energy came back eventually, and I rewarded my tired body with a lot of water. I could feel the withdrawals beginning, a gathering of misery like clouds massing on the horizon. I got on the trail again, taking the left-hand turn marked Kapala'oa Cabin, my first stop.

The trail was flat now, but there were two more miles, and the sand was still deep and soft. I breathed, and walked, and throbbed, my eyes on the fine volcanic gray dust my boots sank into. Periodically I would put my butt up against a boulder and rest the backpack's weight on it and pant for a while, taking sips of water. The arc of sky had flamed with sunset deepening to rose and then purple by the time I finally spotted the cabin ahead.

It was a little, square, surprisingly modern-looking building, and in front of it was a verdant patch of green plushy grass like an oasis. As I got closer, I could see that the grass was nurtured by a spigot, and chuckling and cooing in gentle snorting commentary were a pair of nene geese.

They approached me fearlessly, these beautiful endangered birds, cocking their heads, blinking shiny chocolate eyes to check on my intentions. I collapsed onto the grassy patch, immobilized by tiredness, and they circled me, clacking their beaks sympathetically. A soft buff like a soldier's waistcoat, they were barred in black and cream with pearly gray breasts.

I unlatched the belt and the backpack loosened, and I took my arms out of it. I was here, where I would be for the next four days.

I unlaced the boots, rubbed my wounded toes in the verdant grass, which looked mowed—and I saw why as the nene went back to grazing, plucking blades of grass and eating them with the delicacy of dandies.

I walked barefoot to the water and ran it, clear and icy, over my red, hot, sore feet. When they were sufficiently numb, I padded over to the door of the cabin and plugged the code the rangers had given me into the key box and went inside.

One large room, framed in by walls lined in triple bunks, was bisected by a long wooden table notched with graffiti and scorch marks. The kitchen, off to the left, sported a stove, a sink, and a gas grill. Mismatched melamine plates,

Toby Neal

glasses, and pots were piled in a drainer on the sideboard. A paned window over the sink looked out at the breathtaking view as the sunset flamed along the ridge of a nearby cinder cone.

I hauled the backpack inside. I didn't have to pee, which I knew wasn't a good sign, but I was too tired to do anything but drink the rest of the water I'd carried, take several Advil and a Tylenol, and crawl into my sleeping bag on the lowest bunk of one of the tiers.

I woke sometime in the night.

It was dark, so dark I couldn't see anything with my hand held up to my face.

I finally had to pee, and I had the shakes—maybe from withdrawal, maybe from the chill that slid over my feet like cold oatmeal as I put them outside the chemical-smelling, brand-new sleeping bag.

I felt around for the backpack and found the thick socks that hadn't worked for hiking. I put them on and came across the tiny flashlight the woman at Sports Authority had stuck in my cart.

The flash blasted the darkness away with a high-powered

white beam that made me blink with its ferocity. I had spotted the outhouse near the main cabin, so I padded to the door and opened it.

Stars flamed fiercely across the nearby sky.

Wow, Constance said. I remembered how she'd always loved the night sky, taking the side in our bedroom against the window and making sure her bed was right underneath it. She'd fall asleep looking out the window every night.

It was her idea to reach my hand up, feeling in that velvet darkness for the diamonds that were so close—but of course my fingers just got cold. I pushed my heavy, sore, leaden legs to walk to the outhouse. I went inside its tiny musty space, applying my bare rear to the chill plastic rim of the hole with a little hiss of breath.

I did my business and remembered I had not brought TP and had to pack out my waste. I shone the flashlight around inside the enclosure and discovered a small stash of paper napkins held down by a rock. I tore a square off, used it, and feeling rebellious, dropped it into the hole. I wasn't ready to carry that back to the cabin and figure out how to dispose of it.

Back in the cabin, I felt a thirst begin, my tissues crying

out for water and more—but I'd used up all the clean water
I had. I took a measured hit of vodka and immediately felt
myself relaxing. I got into the sleeping bag and fell back
into the dark.

Chapter 8

I woke with the cottony lip-cracking of dehydration, the gray wash of dawn rendering everything in the cabin the colors of angst. I got out of the sleeping bag reluctantly, feeling every screaming overused muscle from yesterday's hike. I tried not to think about it. Now was the time to "get 'er done," as my mom used to say.

I'd had a lot of "get 'er done" when I was younger, propelling me through college and grad school while working as a waitress. There hadn't been extra money after my parents' divorce. I hadn't had the silver spoon the ex had—a good thing since silver spoons are dated and not a part of my future.

A closet off the kitchen turned out to be stacked high with Pres-to-Logs. Even I could get the stove going with those. I put a log into the wood burner, checked the flue was open, and lit it with the barbeque lighter I found.

After it seemed to be going and there was some promise that the cabin would eventually warm up enough that I wasn't seeing my breath, I turned my attention to the mysterious propane grill. It was time to figure out the stove.

I hadn't used one of these since Richard and I used to go camping back in college. We had a gas barbeque at Hidden Palms, but I didn't remember ever lighting it. Grilling had been Richard's purview.

A white tank rested under the sink, with a handle on it. I turned that on, then turned the dial on the wrought-iron burner, punctuated with a hundred tiny gas-emitting holes. I stuck the barbeque lighter in its general direction and recoiled from the explosion that burst into the air above the stove.

I swear it singed my eyebrows. The flame settled into a blue, obedient circle.

"Note to self. Don't open the valve all the way." I said aloud. I found a big black pot and turned the lever over the sink. Water so cold and clear it burned poured out to fill the pot. I put it on the stove.

There was really nothing to do now until it boiled, which could take a while. I hauled the backpack into the kitchen and unloaded all my food supplies onto the counter, lingering over the coffee and one-cup drip basket I'd brought from home. Yes, it looked like I'd have enough coffee for only one cup a day for the week, but that cup was going to taste so good—and I could have two if I reused the grounds.

I could feel a headache beginning at the base of my punished spine. It was rising with slowness and inevitability toward my eyeballs. I got out the large bottle of Advil I'd also brought. There was nothing to take them with until the water boiled—but the vodka.

I might as well enjoy my last sips—the pint bottle I'd bought at the Liquor Barn was down to half.

I unzipped the sleeping bag and wrapped it around me, stepping outside into the clear morning.

The cabin was snuggled against the precipitous wall of the vast crater, and the floor of it spread before me. To the east, the sun bloomed, a warming bonfire striking the rugged, unworn, jagged volcanic ridge across the valley floor with rich red gold. The air was so thin and pure, I could hear nothing—absolutely nothing—but the rattle of my own tired lungs. Then, ever so far away, I heard the honk of flying nene.

My companions of the day before had flown, leaving little brown piles of scat and a lawn as well trimmed as a golf green. I put four Advil into my mouth and washed them down with vodka.

I swear I meant that to be all I drank, but the next time I looked at the bottle, it was because nothing was left.

But I felt good. Loose in the legs, optimistic. I was going to be cold turkey after this, but it was okay. It was going to be like a spiritual retreat—I'd figure out everything I wanted from life, and I'd visualize it, and it would manifest, like that pop psychology book *The Secret* promised. I was vibrating at the highest level of the universe. I was going to attract joy, health, prosperity, and love into my life.

I squinched my eyes shut, visualizing hard.

I went back into the cabin as the sunrise dissipated itself into the glory of full day in Haleakala Crater.

The giant pot of water was boiling, and had been for some time. I turned it off, relishing the warmth from the stove. My empty belly was awash with vodka and Advil, and I didn't need water or food. I crawled back into bed to enjoy my last alcohol buzz for a week at least, and hopefully the rest of my life.

Chapter 9

The next time I woke, I could tell by the sharp shape of the shadows in the cabin that it was evening. I sat up. Headache. Dry mouth. I went into the kitchen and wrestled the pot to the sink, poured the cool, boiled water into a series of abandoned water bottles from under the sink. No need for refrigeration—all I had to do was put them outside the door.

I drained one of the bottles and poured more water over the dehydrated prunes the Sports Authority woman had recommended "to keep things moving." While they soaked, I took a big piece of jerky outside.

The valley was the same, but the angle of the light was different. That was about all the change this place ever saw on a daily basis.

I meditated on that awhile and considered whether it was too late in the day for coffee. Decided it wasn't: time was a construct used by people who had to keep a schedule, and I no longer did.

I made that cup of coffee, ate the jerky, and the body was temporarily appeased. I had brought my phone, useless now, but it had a camera in it. I put the boots back on and walked carefully and gently down a meandering path that led to one of the cinder cones.

I climbed it and watched the most spectacular sunset I'd ever seen do a wild, heavenly lightshow in a blaze of Technicolor drama, unfettered by anything so mundane as smog, vog, or fog. It made me dizzy and hurt my eyes, but I took a couple of totally inadequate phone pictures anyway.

Cold and approaching dark finally drove me back toward the cabin—and as I tromped along, I realized there wasn't going to be anyone waiting for me there, fixing dinner, lighting the stove. No Hector, even, with his questioning tail. No one knew where I was.

I was truly alone for the first time in my life.

Terror stole the breath from my lungs. I felt invisible,

as if I'd never really existed and didn't really exist now. I found myself lumbering to the cabin at a run, a graceless rapid stumbling with sore legs, big boots, and fear reactivating the awful personal stink.

As that lip-curling stench bloomed around me, it put me back in my body and made me feel real again.

I found myself scanning around the doorway for something left by the stalker—but there was nothing. *This is the beginning of detox; common symptoms are anxiety and paranoia,* Constance reminded me as I climbed the step and took hold of the knob. Still, I wished I'd remembered to carry my pepper spray with me. It was stowed in a side pocket on the backpack.

I opened the door slowly, standing back and ready to run. Of course, the cabin was empty and echoing, only slightly warm from leftover sun and the log I'd burned so many hours ago. I was definitely paranoid—but I wouldn't give in to it and carry the damn pepper spray around, when it was being alone that was scaring me. I got another log going.

I ate the soft-soaked prunes standing at the sink. Drank another quart of water. Put another pot of water on to boil— water was going to be my salvation in the days to come.

Maybe I could even take a bath. That marginally happy idea got me through another joyless trek to the outhouse, this time with a ziplock bag I could use to put the toilet paper in.

Back at the cabin, which was warming up from the wood-burning stove, I stripped to naked at the sink and washed my reeking body with dish soap found under the sink and the blue T-shirt I'd worn, sacrificing it for the duration.

It had been a while since I'd really noticed my body. It wasn't in good shape. I'd always had one of those athletic tennis player builds—tennis being a game I did enjoy—but now my breasts had collapsed into pale little wallets that dangled on my bony rib cage. I'd always had pretty, muscular legs, and this was the first time I ever remembered seeing a gap between my thighs and knees, and the meat of them was jiggly and loose.

I looked like what I knew I'd look like in a rest home if I lived that long—a flask of bones held together with muscle and sinew that were too stubborn to disappear just yet. This was bottom, I reminded myself. I had to get sober before I could get healthy. But I wept as I washed my poor, abused flesh, the skin the color of animal fat rendered to make candles on a farm.

I put on a pair of sweatpants, the thick socks, a sweatshirt. This was my other set of clothes, and it now had to last the rest of the week. It was okay, though. I was clean and ready for the night ahead.

I found a pot to pee in, since constant trips to the out-house through the dark seemed impossible—and realized I was actually using that hackneyed phrase in a real sentence.

I had a pot to pee in. I laughed out loud, and it bounced around the cabin and came back to boomerang off me like a sonar ping. It was the detox, I told myself. I was having a little auditory hallucination.

I had Advil. I had a lineup of bottles of boiled water. I had my sleeping bag, and I was clean. This was as good as it would get. I used the flashlight to read over Kamani's file as I lay in the Naugahyde-covered bunk

I lifted my head. I heard something—a rhythmic crunch-ing sound, like someone was approaching. I switched off the flashlight. I hadn't locked the doors, and that suddenly seemed a ridiculous oversight.

I swung my legs out of the sleeping bag. It was very dark, but I could see the outlines of the windows, limned in moonlight. I crept to the front door, twisted the dead bolt. I heard the steps outside, crunching on the path, as loud as if they were going through the room—then a muffled swishy sound—someone was walking on the grass.

I realized the back door was still unlocked.

I ran across the room and through the kitchen by feel and memory and felt over the surface of the back door, patting it frantic and blind until I felt the parallel knob of the dead bolt and turned it.

Unless they had the ranger code, I was safe.

I crouched below the level of the windows, out of sight, listening. I heard the crunching again, and then the swishing, and then nothing. A series of people were walking by the cabin? The main trail led past it, but it was a bit of a jag to come up to the cabin. I shouldn't be able to hear them.

I heard the steps approaching again, steady and the same tempo as the others. With my eyes adjusted, I was pretty sure I'd be able to see whoever it was. I stood cautiously and looked out through the kitchen windowpanes. The moon was high, and the desert floor of the crater was bathed in otherworldly light. The steps crunched to the front of the cabin and then swished by where I stood, moving on past the window through the grass.

No one was there.

The scene before me was starkly, beautifully empty, moonlight brazing the outlines of every stone, rock, and blade of grass. I remembered the night marchers, a Hawaiian legend of warriors slain in battle who walked the land at night in a ghostly reenactment.

I must be hallucinating.

The hairs all over my body had risen and I trembled, perspiration springing up under my armpits to sully my clean sweatshirt. *This is not acceptable*, Constance said. *You're going to need something stronger than Advil to get through the night.*

I turned on the flash and dug in the backpack, found my Advil bottle, shook out the brown glossy pellets until I found several big, white Vicodin hiding in the bottom.

I took two, tossing them back with a swallow of water, climbed into my sleeping bag, and clamped my eyes shut, wishing I had earplugs or a pillow to wrap around my head. I had neither, and the night marchers passed by with terrible regularity until my friend Vicodin dragged me under into sleep.

I drank that first cup of coffee in the pearly predawn of

day three. My brain felt spongy, like a computer with a

virus, glitching and rebooting whenever it felt like it. The

act of thinking reminded me of the hunt-and-peck typing of

my master's thesis so long ago on an old Olympia: *current*

trends in attribution of attractiveness to facial structures in

males.

I still remembered how hard it had been to come up with

something scientific-sounding to describe that early fascina-

tion I'd had with handsome men—a thesis that had ended

with a close-up anatomical study of Richard. His cheek-

bones, bold jaw, crystalline blue eyes under symmetrical

brow ridges . . . His beauty had intersected with my attribu-

tion of positive characteristics to his looks. I saw that now.

I'd always had a keen aesthetic sense, and it carried me

past my ruminations as my bruised-feeling eyes wandered

over the sweep of crater before me. I could almost see the

molecules of the air warming before me—the heat of the

rising sun making them vibrate faster, light reflecting on

minuscule particles of matter, capturing the process and

transmuting it into bands of yellow and pink that brightened

the stark sky.

A gentle honking, increasing in volume, heralded the

return of my nene friends—but I didn't believe it was really them until I saw their graceful black arcs against the morning sky. They hove in and splashed down on the lush patch of grass in front of the cabin, trotting toward me, folding their wings and chuckling a greeting.

"Hi, guys." The nene bobbed their heads, sidling toward the water spigot and pantomiming drinking. I got up, turned it on for them and watched them paddling their beaks in the drops, lifting their heads so the water ran down their graceful throats.

Knowing about delirium tremens was definitely not the same as experiencing it. This morning my skin was exquisitely tender, and the thousands of tiny fibers of my clothing felt rough as sharkskin. Tiny spiders were crawling over me, and I looked, for the hundredth time, at my arms. Still nothing there since the last time I looked two minutes ago.

I needed to do something today, get out, get my mind off the night that didn't bear remembering and my current problem with crawlies. The nene dipped their heads, making gentle commentary as they finished drinking. One of them sampled the edge of my sleeping bag, cocked his head at me.

"No food," I said, startled by the volume of my voice. "I got nothing for you, guys."

They seemed to accept this and walked away, grazing. The dawn gilded their feathers.

I went back inside the cabin. My paranoia was still pretty bad—I felt like someone was watching me, and I couldn't stop myself from checking under the beds, in the Pres-to-Log closet, outside the back door.

Perhaps what I could do for a project was make a video log with my phone of this whole thing—something I could play when I was tempted to drink again. A note to self from "detoxing me" to "tempted to drink" me. I was semi-shocked my brain had enough juice left in it to come up with such a great idea.

I turned the phone on. As usual there was no signal, but I set it on the battered table and sat in front of it on video mode. Talked to my future self.

"Caprice, you're a wreck. You've been given another chance at life. You've just been through the longest, darkest, scariest night of your life. Auditory hallucinations—the night marchers went by this cabin like clockwork all night long. Paranoia. Anxiety. The shakes. Right now you've got

skin hallucinations." I held my arm up in front of the blinking camera. "See the chicken skin? Something's crawling on
me right now."

I looked into that ruthless camera eye. "I'm doing it. I'm
suffering right now so you, me in the future, can have a better life. Don't fuck it up."

I reached over and hit Off.

This was just what I needed. Making this video was the
perfect project for the day.

I shot footage of the cabin, the bottles of water, my
precious Advil bottle. I took off my clothes in front of the
warm woodstove and shot video of my ravaged body. Then
I put the clothes and boots back on, drank my second cup
of coffee (much weaker as I reused the grounds), and with
some prunes, jerky, and a granola bar, I set off down a side
trail to see what I could explore.

Kapala`oa Cabin is not the farthest cabin out, but it's far
enough to make things interesting in terms of nearby trails,
which meandered in various directions from the main trail
turnoff. I walked down the path I knew I'd need to take the
day after tomorrow to Holua Cabin, the one I'd be staying
in for three more days.

So far, I hadn't met any other people hiking even though the ranger had said there was a fair amount of foot traffic through the crater.

I soon left the scrubby grass behind and entered a sweep of astral pebbles, littered with boulders that looked like they'd fallen from space. Cinder cones jutted around me like terrestrial boils, their steep contoured sides streaked with a range of colors from umber to purple. I paused to shoot little video panoramas, even picking up a handful of bright orange pumice, edges of stone light and sharp as my grandmother's handmade lace. I videoed the pumice in my hand.

One of my grandmothers had been Swedish, and that crocheted lace she did was amazing. I'd always wanted to learn how.

No, you didn't, Constance said. *You always were more interested in people.*

Constance was still piping up, with her unique and powerful voice. I'd kept her silent for so long—but in my physical and emotional extremity, I found her strength, her definite opinions comforting.

"You always knew what to do, Constance," I murmured aloud. "Even when it was a bad idea."

A vivid memory came to me—the time when we were six and Constance decided we should do a "twin" song-and-dance performance for the school talent show. I'd coped by pretending I was Constance, and still I'd flubbed the words and tripped over my feet. That was the beginning of my rebellion against Constance's stream of ideas for the two of us.

I hadn't been sure who I was, but I'd been sure I wasn't her.

I stopped and turned the video on. The sun was filling the crater with powdered light, and the crawlies seemed to have been dispelled by gentle exercise. A nearby cinder cone cast a sharp, deep shadow, and I stepped into it. Immediately, the air was at least ten degrees cooler.

"Shadow," in Jungian psychology, is where all the dark, scary, forbidden things about oneself are hidden—and in a healthy psyche, those things are known and accepted. In an unhealthy one, they are denied. I'd been unhealthily denying all the parts of me that were Constance.

About time you realized that, Constance said. *I'm so sorry. I never wanted to leave you.*

Tears prickled my eyes. I stood with my body in the

shadow and shone the video eye on my sunlit face. "I never grieved properly for my twin, my beloved sister, Constance. I never acknowledged how the loss of her shaped everything about my life and my career. I never acknowledged the guilt that I lived and she died—when she was so much more than me. And because of that, the tiny bit of relief I felt that she was gone. Oh God."

I felt more tears rising up, and I turned off the phone camera and let them come. I folded up into the shadow of the vast cone and wept for her, feeling her nearby, touching my hair, a welcome tactile hallucination.

Finally, feeling emptied out and shaky, I pushed myself up and headed back toward the cabin. Walking along the fairly even trail, unburdened by the backpack, I was able to let my mind wander over the path of my life—a choice to become someone who was more of an observer than a participant.

Not that I hadn't done good work, hadn't made a difference. I knew I had. But I also knew I'd always played it safe, taken the path of least resistance, and turned away from anything that reminded me of Constance. I was tired and emotionally drained, my legs and lungs still overworked, as I headed back to the cabin. I anticipated drinking a quart of water and taking a nap.

What I didn't anticipate was a visitor.

Chapter 10

A man was sitting on the top step of the cabin. He was dark, with the overgrown hair of the young and hirsute, and even seated I could see he was enormously tall. The overlong bones of a giant protruded from the sleeves of his anorak, ending in hands the size of baseball mitts. He wore thick glasses, and he pushed them up his nose before he addressed me.

"I believe there's been some mistake. I have a reservation for this cabin."

"Hello," I said, my voice rusty. I wasn't even sure he was real at this point. "Who are you?"

"Russell Pruitt." He stood. I backed up, almost stumbling.

He was at least seven feet tall, and he'd unfolded in sections like one of those foldable yardsticks. "I'm hiking Haleakala. I got here, plugged in my code to the door, and I see you're already settled in."

"Oh." My brain refused to compute. What a bizarre coincidence—or was it a coincidence? "Russell Pruitt." I felt overcome by thirst and dizziness. "I need some water. I think I'm a little dehydrated."

I brushed past him to the interior. One glance told me Russell Pruitt had moved my backpack; it was turned toward the door, my cabin permit clearly clipped to it. He followed me in, and his head bent a little to accommodate the nearby ceiling.

"I was looking for who you were, Dr. Wilson, and if you were supposed to be here," he said, his tone apologetic. "I can see you are supposed to be here, but so am I."

"Oh," I said again, heading for the sink and the water. I took one of my bottles, unscrewed the top, guzzled. My sluggish brain ticked over this new, very unwelcome information.

Choices: I could share the space with my new roommate. I could pack everything up and go to the next cabin—but it wasn't "mine" for another two days. I could hike out of the crater, if I had the strength, and abort Mission Detox.

None of the above appealed.

"I'm okay with just staying together," Russell Pruitt said. His voice was unusually deep and had a vibration like a cello. "I'm a journalist. I'm doing a story on the crater. I'm not going to be around the cabin much, anyway."

"I don't know," I said, turning back to him. His dark eyes were glittery and bright behind those Coke-bottle glasses, and his height was unnerving. I noticed he had dark olive skin and wondered what ethnicity of giant he was. "I'm on a retreat. I hadn't planned on being around other people. No offense." I mentally composed my scathing complaint to the Park Service.

"Well, I'm taking this bunk." He gestured with one ham hand to a bunk across the room. His backpack already leaned against it, a down sleeping bag rolled out on the bed.

"Okay. I guess that's how it's going to be, then. I've been ill and had a bad night; I'm going to take a nap now." I spoke in the firm, forthright voice I used with clients and headed for my bunk.

"Okay. I'm sorry about this." Russell Pruitt sounded

downcast, like a Great Dane smacked with a newspaper. It occurred to me he was very young, probably around my son's age, but the height thing threw off any normal assessment of him.

"Me too," I said. I took off my boots and climbed into my sleeping bag, clamping my eyes shut. He was silent a long moment. I imagined he must be looking at me, wondering at my awful color, my socially bizarre behavior—but quite frankly, I didn't have the energy to do anything but lie down at the moment.

I heard the creak of the boards of the floor as his massive bulk moved to the door, the squeak of the hinges as he opened it, the *thunk* as it closed, the *snick* of the latch tongue finding the notch in the doorframe.

I was rattled. I brought my phone up out of my pocket and shone its blinking camera eye down on my face as I lay on my pillowless bunk. "In a strange twist of events in this documentary, I am now sharing the cabin with Russell Pruitt, a young journalist giant," I whispered. "I'm not looking forward to making social niceties with him feeling the way I do."

I turned the phone off, ever mindful of my battery, and

settled my arms beside myself, breathing deeply and prac-
ticing some progressive relaxation to help me nap.

I must have fallen asleep, but the waking was sudden and
abrupt. A thought had occurred to me and was so urgent I
woke up with it burning in my mind: I hadn't actually seen
his permit, nor introduced myself as Dr. Wilson.

I thought of what information was on the permit clipped
onto my backpack—and I was virtually sure my title of
"Doctor" wasn't listed. I was simply Caprice Wilson for
purposes of this trip.

How had he known I was Dr. Wilson?

I got out of the sleeping bag and tiptoed over to the permit, folded and dangling from the pack in its plastic sleeve.
I slid it out, unfolded it. Ah, there it was where my name
was listed: "Caprice Wilson, PhD."

Habit. I'd filled it in with my title since I did that on all
my case and other notes. But it wasn't displayed on the part
that was exposed by the fold for rangers to check, which
meant he'd taken the paper out, looked at my home address.
Looked at my emergency contact information. Looked at
my length of stay and that I was at Holua Cabin next.

What the hell was this guy up to? Was my paranoia just

returning? Still, better safe than sorry, and I couldn't do anything to deal with the situation in my sick and weakened state—better just to get my pepper spray and go back to bed, rest, think about what to do and if I was paranoid or if Russell Pruitt was a real danger. I felt in the side pocket, removing the small first aid kit—and there was nothing else there.

My pocketknife was gone. My pepper spray was gone.

I scrabbled through the side pocket, as if looking repeatedly would make it appear. I turned the backpack upside down—there wasn't much left inside, the dirty yoga pants, a few odds and ends. I searched through every single pocket and zip.

My two weapons were gone.

I sat on the floor and felt a wave of panic rise up through my body to choke me. My heart thundered, a bass drum. I panted like I'd run a marathon. Perspiration burst out all over me, instantly soaking my sweatshirt and hair. I gasped, vainly sucking for oxygen as I battled the urge to scream.

I must be having a panic attack. I remembered a first aid pamphlet that said to cough hard to get the heart going again, but with my mouth wide and hyperventilating, I couldn't seem to get enough breath to cough.

I had to get outside. Outside, under the bowl of sky, nothing could be that bad. I crawled to the door, took the handle in both hands, twisted. It wouldn't open. I pushed; I leaned; I pounded; I twisted. Something was wrong with the door.

I gasped and coughed. Kept coughing until it turned to dry heaves.

I felt like I was dying. My first panic attack was way scarier than I'd ever known. My words to clients echoed in my addled mind: "Panic attacks occur when the limbic system is activated by a real or imagined threat. Adrenaline and cortisol flood the nervous system, causing a fight-or-flight response. If fight or flight is not possible, the body seems to turn on itself, short-circuiting with the overload."

My fight-or-flight was blocked, and I'd never make light of this experience again in my work, I told myself—if I got out of this situation alive.

Maybe the back door was open. I stood up and ran to it, twisted the handle. It turned, but nothing else happened. I pushed, twisted, yanked, and pounded.

Russell Pruitt had taken my weapons and locked me in the cabin.

Chapter 11

*D*r. Wilson." His deep, measured voice came from the front door. I noticed again its timbre, like it came up from some deep, booming well. I pictured his barrel chest, huge lungs, enlarged larynx. "I'm sorry. I can tell you aren't well, and I wouldn't do this if I didn't badly need your services."

I walked back into the front room, stroking my arms as one soothes a cat because the crawling sensations had returned with a vengeance. Services? Russell Pruitt had locked me into the cabin because he wanted therapy?

I was stuck in the wilderness where literally no one knew where I was, with a crazy giant. The part of me that still had a sense of humor appreciated the bizarreness of it all.

"I have to pee," I said, because it was the truth.

A long pause as Russell Pruitt considered this. "Use a pot. We have to establish trust before I can let you out."

I opened my mouth on a cackle of laughter, closed it again. Establish trust? That showed how delusional he was. I needed to get my psychologist hat on, and fast.

I found my pot from the night before, dropped my pants, peed into it. Squatting on that aluminum container, I looked around the kitchen. Surely there was something useful here somewhere. My eyes scanned the windows—small panes of glass framed in metal, they were riveted into their frames. Breaking one would only turn the steel frames into bars.

I wiped with a square of paper towel, put the waste in my ziplock bag like a good little camper, stowed the pot under the sink, and began an FBI-level search of the kitchen for something to use as a weapon.

"I took all the sharp objects out of the kitchen," Russell Pruitt said from outside. "It's okay. You're safe with me."

I ignored this, continuing to search, my mind shuddering at the thought of Russell Pruitt's enormous hands—just one of them was big enough to crack my skull like an egg. It didn't bear thinking of.

The only thing I could find was the extra stove lighter, a bulb of lighter fluid with a striker on the end that made a flame when the trigger was pulled. Maybe I could stick it in his eye or something.

"I'm getting cold out here. I'm going to come in, and I want you to get back into your sleeping bag so we can talk," Russell Pruitt said. "I'm going to fix us some dinner. You'll like it."

"And if I don't want to get back into my sleeping bag?" I said, holding the barbeque lighter aloft, bemused by its uselessness.

"I'll put you in there myself. It'll take longer for us to get to know each other," he said in his pedantic way. The thought of him stuffing me into my sleeping bag had me hyperventilating again. It was unfair that I'd been ambushed at my lowest point mentally and physically, but I was a savvy psychologist who'd dealt with hundreds of psychopaths and criminals in my time.

I just needed to outwit him; that was all.

If I could escape somehow, I'd need my boots.

"Okay," I said meekly. "I want to at least hear what you

have in mind." As if I had a choice. I shoved my feet into the boots and swung my legs up to my sleeping bag, stuck them inside, climbed in, and zipped myself up. I tucked the lighter along with the flashlight down into my sweatpants. "I'm in."

Russell Pruitt opened the door and entered, bending his enormous head because he barely cleared the ceiling. He looked over at me, cocooned in my bag.

"Good. We can get started." He carried his backpack back in and took out a screwdriver and a tongue-and-hasp combination. Walked back to the door and began screwing the hasp side on. He was putting a lock on the door.

I felt terror rising up again, but I did a couple of calming breaths and focused on engaging him.

"You've said you want to establish trust with me. I'm wondering how putting a lock on the inside of the door is going to help me trust you," I said, with the warm tone of neutral curiosity I used to help clients explore conflicting goals. "Locking the door sends a message that I'm a prisoner, and neither of us is to be trusted."

"Aha. Motivational interviewing," Russell Pruitt said, correctly identifying my technique, his back massive as a wall as he put heft into turning the screws. "I wondered what your opening gambit would be. Nice try, Dr. Wilson, but I'm not actually a journalist. I'm a psychology grad student."

"Interesting." I fumbled my phone up, hit the video button, aimed it at him from beside me. I wanted to record some of this—for law enforcement or posterity, whichever came first. "If so, you must be aware that taking me captive to do therapy is a flawed scenario. The unconditional positive regard and trust necessary to the therapeutic process are compromised."

Russell Pruitt turned back, the screwdriver tiny in his fist. I hoped he didn't see the edge of the camera phone poking up with its blinking red RECORD eye. "I needed to see you. It's a matter of life and death."

I took a moment to absorb this—his face was very pale, and greasy sweat had sprung up along his hairline as his eyes shone with feverish, glassy light. I wasn't the only one who looked ill. Something besides delusion was going on with him—something physical. I seemed to remember gigantism was caused by tumors on the pituitary gland and that many giants didn't live long due to enlarged organs.

"Two questions. No one knew I was coming here. How did you find me? And why didn't you just make an appointment?"

Russell Pruitt, if that was indeed his name, walked back over to his backpack, slid the screwdriver inside, and took out a combination lock. He walked back to the front door, pulled the tongue over the hasp, hooked the steel lock through the eye, and clicked it shut with a final-sounding click. I almost moaned aloud—and bit my lips instead.

"I'll answer your questions after I make dinner," he said. He walked back over to his backpack and reached in to take out a silvery cold pack bag. "I brought all your favorite things." He shook the bag, as if displaying doggie treats to a hound, and went into the kitchen.

I stayed silent, my brain scrabbling. How had he found me here? Literally, no one knew where I'd gone after I got off the plane in Maui. It doesn't matter how he found me, I told myself. What mattered was that I begin to take control of the situation and find a way to escape. I turned the phone off, slid it back into my pocket. I sat up, pushing the sleeping bag down around my waist—still technically obeying him, but concealing my boots.

His back was turned and he was chopping something in the kitchen. "You haven't been eating well lately, Dr. Wilson. You've lost weight."

"I know. I've been ill."

"No. You've been drinking."

I narrowed my eyes at the back of his enormous head. He had to be the stalker. There was no other answer. He must have been observing me. I clamped down on my millions of questions. I needed to stay on task. "I think it's much more interesting to find out about *you*. What is this matter of life and death?"

"You like pasta with shrimp and cream sauce," he said, as if I hadn't spoken. "It's amazing you've kept your figure all these years. Anyway, I thought you'd be ready for a really good meal after being down here a few days."

"Thank you for being so considerate." He was already showing me what he would and wouldn't do. "I've read gigantism is a tough diagnosis. Many people with the disorder don't make it out of their twenties due to health complications. Is that what's happening to you?"

"I also brought asparagus," he said. I saw the flash of the big butcher knife that used to be in the dish rack, heard it whack the cutting board with excessive force, making me jump. I looked around, wondering if I could sneak over to his backpack and search it while his back was turned. As if he read my mind, he turned, and the waning light of evening glanced off the blade, rendered tiny by his hand.

"You aren't lying down."

"You didn't say I had to. I'm in my sleeping bag. I'm following directions," I said softly.

He turned back and resumed chopping, then filled a pot with boiled water, turning to the stove. Good. He'd let me get away with something. I could build on that progressively until I gained the upper hand. He had some sort of respect or regard for me; I would use that authority to strengthen my position.

I had left the second striker near the stove, anticipating that he'd miss it if I took the only one—and now he lit the burner without comment even as I wondered how the hell the hidden striker was ever going to help me.

"Now a drink. You must be feeling terrible by now, when you'd been drinking so much daily." He lifted a bottle of Grey Goose, my favorite vodka, off the counter, waggled it, and poured at least five fingers into a plastic cup.

My whole body tightened, and I felt my mouth fill with saliva. I was Pavlov's dog incarnate, hardly human in the violent wave of longing that swept me. I shuddered with the power of it as he approached me, holding the full plastic cup in two hands like it was the Holy Grail.

"No, thank you," I said feebly. "I've been cutting back."

"I know you have. You've been very brave, trying very hard. But I think you've dealt with this wrinkle in your plans admirably, and you deserve a reward." Russell Pruitt held out the yellow plastic cup of clear, odorless liquid. I held my quivering hands still in my lap to restrain them from taking it. I realized that, no matter how much I wanted that drink, I didn't want it even more.

"Thanks so much, Russell Pruitt, but I just couldn't."

"Oh, but I insist." Then followed a brief flurry of violence in which he sat on my bunk, lifted me like a doll over his legs, held me down, and pinched my nostrils. When I gasped for breath, he poured the vodka into my throat until I choked and swallowed. He then sat me up and handed me the cup.

"Drink," he said. "Or we'll keep doing that until it's gone."

I drank. When the cup was empty, I handed it to him.

He patted my tousled hair. "Now, isn't that better?"

And horribly, revoltingly, I had to admit that it was—even as tears streamed down my cheeks. The heat of the liquor ignited in my belly, ran like liquid energy down my arms and legs, and every deprived circuit in my body and brain wanted to leap up and sing "hallelujah." For some reason, I thought of Bruce, his hard brown eyes challenging me. How angry he'd be that I hadn't gone to Aloha House. The tears wouldn't stop pouring down my cheeks.

"No means no, Russell Pruitt. I said no, and I feel violated by you making me drink that."

"I think we need to suspend some of the social niceties for the duration," he said. "I'm sorry you felt violated." He got up and went back into the kitchen.

He'd very effectively shown me how strong he was and asserted total domination over me. I felt queasy with fear and the huge shot of vodka.

"So, what do you know about sociopaths?" he asked conversationally, stirring the pot of pasta.

"Quite a lot, actually," I said. What was he getting at? The booze was working, loosening my tongue and the tight joints of my hips and knees, falsely restoring my confidence by expanding the constriction of my cerebral cortex. Knowing that was happening didn't make it less effective. "Why do you want to know?"

He didn't answer that. "Do you think the diagnosis of psychopathy should be admitted to the DSM-V in lieu of antisocial personality disorder? Many psychologists and psychiatrists in the profession are divided over this."

"Sociopathology refers to a pattern of antisocial behaviors and is recorded Axis Two, but the group submitting the psychopathy definition have done neurological MRI studies showing that the brains of psychopaths don't process emotion the way normal people do. That group wants to have a psychopathic disorder available on Axis One, the main diagnostic axis."

"You didn't tell me what your opinion was." His back was turned at the stove.

"I'm not a part of the committee reviewing the submissions, but I think there's merit in having that diagnosis available." I leaned back against the wall so that the upper bunk would shield me from his view. "Why are you asking?"

He didn't reply.

I brushed the tears from my cheeks, hoping that one drink wouldn't make me have to go through withdrawals again—but if he made me keep drinking, I'd be right back at ground zero. What a horrible form of abuse, and it scared me down to my untied boots.

He was cooking shrimp in a frying pan, and it smelled delicious. I was disgusted by how hungry I was, how much better I felt after he'd fed me the drink. *You might have to do a lot worse to stay alive before you get away than eat shrimp and drink booze,* Constance said. *You can feel guilty later.*

A thought occurred to me—maybe Aloha House would call Bruce and tell him that I'd never arrived, and he'd be worried. Kamani too. And Bruce might call Chris, and Chris would tell him I was on Maui and that I'd always wanted to hike Haleakala, that Richard and I had always planned to, and they'd figure out where I'd gone. It was a dim hope, but a real one.

Someone might come looking for me. Someone might take it seriously that I'd disappeared, even if it was because of my own stupidity. One call to the ranger station, and they'd know I was in Haleakala Crater.

And then they'd wait for me to come out of the crater. No one was going to come looking for me down here until my permit expired, at least four more days.

The feeling of hope dying felt so bad I wished I'd never had it in the first place.

"Dinner's ready," Russell Pruitt said. He carried two steaming plates of pasta and shrimp to the table along with a battery-operated lamp.

I was still ashamed of my hunger but resigned as I kept the sleeping bag over my legs and transferred myself to the bench in front of the battle-scarred table.

"Mmm. Smells delicious," I said, and meant it.

"Good. We'll start therapy after dinner," Russell Pruitt said. "Eat up. You'll need your strength."

Chapter 12

I got back onto my bunk after dinner, my booted feet still hidden in the sleeping bag.

"It's good to get comfortable for our talk, Russell. Not too many places to sit—why don't you just lie down on your bunk?"

He appeared to think this over, a crease appearing between black untamed brows as he collected the plates. His features showed some of the characteristics of gigantism— a protruding forehead with prominent brow ridges, a vast underslung jaw. My brain finally supplied the medical name for his condition: acromegaly.

His grayish color was a little better after eating (I'd had a bowl of the pasta, and he'd eaten the remainder of the pot), and he'd drunk a quart or so of water as well. I reminded myself he'd hiked down the Sliding Sands today. Russell Pruitt had to be getting tired.

"It's my habit to take notes while we talk. Is that all right?" I asked. I wanted to establish my authority position again after the drinking incident. Taking notes and listening was also where I felt most comfortable.

"Of course." Russell Pruitt set the dishes in the sink, ran water over them, and lumbered to his bunk. He folded himself into its short, narrow space, lying on his side, those glassy-bright eyes on me as I picked up the folder with Freitas's profiles inside.

"I'll just use the back of these papers here."

"I'm interested in what you think of those profiles," he said. "They must be suspects in a case of yours." How had he had time to so thoroughly search my things?

"It's a consultation," I said carefully, lifting my knees and setting the folder on them to write. "Confidential. This is *your* time. Now, you said this was a matter of life and death."

"Yes. A matter of my life and your death," Russell Pruitt

replied.

"Hmm," I said, writing "making veiled threats" on the paper. "That sounds serious. Tell me about what's brought this on." My heart beat triple speed, and the vodka and pasta weren't mixing well. I belched, hoping I wasn't going to vomit.

"I've got some health issues. I need to sort them out, come to some conclusions."

"The stakes clearly couldn't be higher. Why don't you tell me where this all began for you." I needed to keep him talking as long as possible, and keep him liking and respecting me. Hopefully I could drag the therapy out until someone came looking for me—four more days. The thought made my bladder loosen.

"I found out I had gigantism when I was thirteen. Can you imagine what it's like to be a normal kid, then suddenly find yourself six feet tall within just a few months?"

"No, I can't imagine," I said honestly. "Tell me more about what that was like."

"I was in unspeakable pain because my bones and sinews grew too fast. I have stretch marks in my skin." He pushed up a sleeve so I could see striations lining the insides of his arms, like the laddering of a snag in a nylon stocking. "I was teased and picked on. The bullies all wanted to fight me because I was so big, and I had no idea how to fight."

"You were overwhelmed emotionally by the changes in your body as you grew too fast, and it attracted unwelcome aggressive attention," I said, reflecting back both the content and emotion of his tale. I found myself feeling compassion for this tormented young man; at the same time, I was burning with my own questions: *Why me? Why now? Why this way?*

"Yes, that's it exactly. I became a freak, almost overnight, and it came at a very bad time for me." He closed his eyes in a long pause, and I couldn't wait any longer.

"That must have been terrible, and I want to know everything about what led you to this point. But earlier in the evening, I had two questions for you, and you said you'd answer them after we ate. I'm still wondering about those questions. Do you remember what they were?"

"I do." Russell Pruitt rolled onto his back, his blue-jeaned legs folded and still so long the tops of his knees brushed the underside of the top bunk. "It's all part of the story. I'll answer the easiest one first. I tracked your cell phone. I hacked your carrier, bought a phone tracker app, and had it ping your phone's location. I knew everywhere you went, and I knew when it went off the grid at the top of Haleakala. I knew you must have hiked in. The only gamble was which cabin you'd headed for, but this one was the most logical choice for someone not in the greatest shape physically."

"Oh," I said, feeling deflated by this practical solution to what had seemed an impenetrable puzzle. "So you have some computer skills too."

"I'm very good. If only curing myself could be done on computer."

"What's wrong with you, exactly?"

"I'm doing all the hormone therapies that are best practice for this syndrome, but damage was done to my heart and internal organs when I was younger and everything was growing too fast. I didn't have parents looking out for me."

"Tell me about that," I said, making a note: "No parents. Hacker. Tracked my cell phone." I realized I was actually very interested in his story.

"I don't think I'm ready to tell you about that. But I will tell you about your clients."

"What about them?" I looked up at him, feeling protectiveness rise up in me.

"I wanted to know what kind of people you saw in your practice. Who thought you were a good enough psychologist to work with. It was an interesting piece of research."

I breathed through a wave of nausea. "How did you do that?"

"Now, if I told you that, I'd have to kill you." He snorted a laugh that sounded boyish and young. But he wasn't a kid, and it wasn't cute. "I particularly like the Southern chick. She's a bit of a psychopath herself, running around stealing stuff with that fluffy hair and the dog. I wanted to take the dog, but he would have been a hassle. I felt sorry for Mrs. Kunia too. Didn't know depression was so prevalent in older people."

"Mrs. Kunia, has had a lot of grief," I said. "Please leave my clients alone. They're just people like you, people trying to work through problems." I thought of the "World's Greatest Grandma" mug. "Did you take items from them and leave them for me to find?"

"That's it exactly."

"Why?"

"I was curious about them, about your practice. I wanted

you to figure out what was going on, but you weren't getting it."

"Like a stalker."

"No, like a psychology student doing fieldwork. Work I wanted to share with you."

"Clients have rights. Their privacy and confidentiality is protected. Studying them because of me—it violates every code of our profession." My voice trembled with conviction and outrage, and I burped again, feeling the shrimp dinner pressing up against my esophagus. I set the folder aside. "I don't feel well. I don't think I'm used to all this rich food. Can we take a break? Can I just sit outside a moment, see if the nausea passes? I don't want to throw up right here."

He turned his head and looked at me a long moment, considering. The sun was long gone, and the dark was palpable beyond the windows. I gulped, trying to settle the roiling of my stomach, and he must have seen my symptoms were real because he got up with frightening swiftness and went to the combination lock, spun it with a memorized combination, and opened the door. A square of starlit liberty gleamed before me, light from the lantern falling on the lush grass in front of the stoop.

I kicked the sleeping bag off and stumbled to the door, wild to get outside and try to run—but as I passed, he caught hold of my hair, bringing me up short with my own momentum. He reached back and picked up my sleeping bag, still holding my hair. My head bent back, my face pulled achingly tight, and tears of pain and disappointment started in my eyes as he walked behind me to the top step, following me down onto the grass.

"Get into your sleeping bag," he said gently. "You might get cold." I also couldn't run with the sleeping bag on. I obeyed, drew it up to my waist. He let go of my hair, a relief so intense it felt like pleasure.

We sat. The nene were gone, back to where they roosted at night, and the stars flamed in a timeless Milky Way rainbow overhead. Russell Pruitt closed the door behind us, and I did some relaxation breathing, calming my nausea, and slowly lay back on the short, thick grass, folding my arms under my head. He did the same, and we both looked at the vast infinity of space.

I was momentarily disoriented, feeling so close to those stars, as if gravity would suspend its bondage and I might fall out into them, drifting away forever among those spinning balls of light and energy. Thin air and no light pollution made me feel like I was on a space station. I reached a hand over to touch the prickly softness of the grass as an anchor.

"I wonder where we go when we die," Russell Pruitt said.

"I wonder too. What do you think about that?"

"I kind of like the idea of living forever," he said, and there was infinite sadness in his big, slow voice. "But I don't believe it."

"Why not?"

"It just seems like a child's wishful thinking, and I'm not a child. I just wish I had longer to figure these things out."

"You've implied several times that this is a matter of life and death and that you didn't have long to figure things out. Tell me what's going on." In the dark, side by side, our conversation took on a new intimacy, as if I were the priest and he in the confessional beside me. It felt comfortable, like he was any other client coming to me for help.

"I'm dying. Congestive heart failure. My heart is enlarged and weak from overexpansion; whole parts of it are dead. The doctors give me a few months to live—and I'm not a candidate for transplant because of the gigantism."

"I've heard there are heart problems with your diagnosis.

I'm so sorry. Getting down to the cabin must have been a tremendous strain." I thought of my own travail. His must have been even worse.

"You have no idea. I had to take nitro when I got here, and rest. Almost didn't make it."

"So that leads me to the second question I asked you before. Why have you followed me? Why not just make an appointment?"

"Because." He sighed, a long slow sigh into the chill night air. "Because I knew I had to confront you at some point with how you'd destroyed my life, and I was worried you'd come down here to commit suicide."

I closed my eyes, unable to really process this—there were too many missing pieces. I racked my brain. Nothing about him—his name, his appearance—was familiar, and yet he seemed to blame me for something. "I wonder how I could have destroyed your life."

He didn't answer.

"You have good instincts," I finally said. "But no. I'm not suicidal." Constance's voice in my head cried, *Denial!*, but I ignored her. Most of me really did want to live. "I came here because I want to get sober. I want to get past my divorce

Unsound 165

and adjust to the empty house with my son, Chris, gone to college."

"Well, that's good, at least."

"It was until you got here. Insisting on therapy." The words popped out before I could stop them, and I could swear they were spoken in Constance's voice.

"All part of what's meant to be, Dr. Wilson."

Another long silence spun out between us, and I thought about how all we are is energy trapped in different forms, subatomic particles vibrating in arbitrary patterns. We're all the same at the particle level, even him and me.

"So you said you wanted to confront me. Why didn't you just make an appointment? I would have been happy to see you. To try to help you."

"I want you to suffer," he said. "I want you to feel the loneliness, fear, and pain I felt. Just a little of it. I wanted you to figure out that I knew everything about you."

I breathed through the surge in my heart rate. "What purpose would that serve?" I said, when I was sure my voice would be coolly interested and nothing more.

"Justice. It's about justice."

What did he mean? I didn't know all the facts—he still

wasn't telling me everything.

"So. Help me understand here." Back to motivational interviewing, a technique for exploring ambivalence and breaking through illogic. "You start 'investigating' me, tracking me. You follow and ambush me and take me prisoner when I'm ill and trying to change my life so you can get some therapy you've decided you need. What part of that is about justice?"

"Shut up!" he yelled. He stood in a surge of mountainous strength, took hold of my sleeping bag, and hauled me back into the cabin, bumping and flailing up the steps. He flung me in the direction of my bunk. I rolled and fetched up against the leg of the bed. I lay there, my cheek against the worn and pockmarked floor, the wind knocked out of me, looking at the dust bunnies hiding deep under the bunk against the wall.

I heard the thump of the front door closing, muttering as he slammed the hasp and lock home, floor-shaking stomps as he went into the kitchen—and then ordinary splashing as he washed the dishes.

I was going to need to go along with his version of reality. I saw that now. This wasn't real therapy, where my job was to gently rattle clients' cages and help them see their lives from a new perspective.

This was keeping the giant happy so I could live another day.

I was afraid to move and was still winded from the back of the step knocking the air out of my lungs as he'd dragged me up them. I slowly turned my head to observe him, but I didn't move otherwise. I wondered how his heart was dealing with the strain of the last few minutes, and in a moment I had my answer—he staggered back across the big room and fell onto his bunk, fumbling for something in his pocket.

"Pills," Russell Pruitt gasped, his face a bluish gray in the pale light of the lantern. "Help me."

Chapter 13

*I*wondered if he would conveniently die while I waited and watched—but if he didn't, he would punish me for not helping. So I moved, but haltingly, as if crippled by pain, pushing myself up in the sleeping bag, unzipping slowly.

He fumbled and gasped, dropping the pill bottle of what I assumed was nitroglycerin, and it landed on the floor and rolled under his bunk.

My eyes on his, I pushed the sleeping bag down and then crawled across the floor toward him, reaching under the bed for the pills. Pressing down hard and twisting the childproof cap, I shook two out into my palm. He opened his mouth like an enormous baby bird, lifting his tongue, and I set the two nitro tablets under it. He closed his mouth and fell back onto the bed, and I crawled away.

It occurred to me that this was my chance to escape, if only I could restrain him, or arm myself, or both. I jumped up and hurried into the kitchen, yanking open one of the drawers for the piece of rope I remembered seeing. I took the big butcher knife out of the dish rack and the piece of rope and ran back to Russell Pruitt.

He was lying on his back, his breath rattling in his lungs, his color still bad. I'd made a loop with the rope, and I slid it over one of his massive hands, an awkward move with the knife in my other hand.

His eyes fluttered open, and I dropped the knife, reaching across him to grab his other hand, pulling them together and wrestling the loop over them. I pulled it tighter, my hands slippery with sweat, and threw the loose end around the tier of the bunk.

He sat up, swinging his tied hands like a baseball bat, and I dodged out of the way, kicking the knife far across the floor, where it skittered under one of the bunks. He surged to his feet, and I danced away around the corner of the bunk, wrapping the rope around the bed support, bracing one foot

on the bunk and pulling with all my might to try to drag him
down and tie him to the bunk.

He roared like a Bengal tiger and yanked with all his
giantness, and the rope ripped through my hands, tearing my
palms. In a few blurred and terrible moments, I was back
in the sleeping bag with the selfsame rope wrapped around
my neck at the top of the bag to seal me in. He'd tied it in
a square knot, just loose enough for me to breathe and no
more. I thought of the scene in *The Hobbit* where all the
dwarves were trussed in bags beside the fire by the trolls. I
wanted to laugh. I must be losing it.

"You're lucky we aren't done with our therapy," he said,
sitting back on his haunches, panting, those oversized hands
hanging between his knees. "Don't try that again."

"Okay," I said.

I woke in the predawn of day four having to pee. I'd slept
very well, trussed like a sausage in my bag. Maybe it was
the dose of booze he'd fed me; maybe it was a whole new
level of tiredness from all the exertions of the day. The night
marchers never appeared, my crawlies were gone, and even
the headache had dissipated. Only a few bruises from hitting

the steps and rope abrasions on my hands hurt today.

If I didn't tell Pruitt that we were supposed to leave for Holua Cabin today, the other campers might come—and I could tell them I was a prisoner. This heartening idea gave me the courage to call across the giant's rumbling snores: "Russell Pruitt. I have to pee. Russell. Pruitt!"

He woke on the last yell and sat up carefully to avoid hitting his head on the bottom bunk. I had a sense he'd had a rough night of it, with at least a foot of him hanging off the end of the bunk.

"What?" he said, rubbing his hand across his face.

"I have to pee."

"You always have to pee."

"I know it seems like that. But I've been drinking a lot of water, trying to flush the booze out."

He came over, untied the knot at my throat.

"How are you feeling?" I asked, looking up at his vast pale face, shadowed with beard stubble and pitted with old acne scars.

"Like you care." He sounded as petulant as my son in his teen years.

"I do care," I said, and was surprised to find it true. For

all his terrible strength, I could see what a boy he was, and I didn't like that he was dying—even as I remembered the butcher knife was still under one of the bunks and I probably should have stabbed him with it yesterday.

"I'll have to take you to the outhouse. Get your pot." He tied the rope around my wrist. "Glad you found this rope for us."

"Yeah, wow, that backfired," I agreed, and was surprised by a snort of a laugh from Pruitt. He followed me as I went into the kitchen.

"Why are you wearing your boots?" he asked, as I got the pee pot out from under the sink.

"Why do you think?" I said.

He shook his big head. "No running. You'll be sorry if you do."

I stood next to him like a dog on a leash as he spun the combination lock, let us out the front door. "I don't want you to kill me."

"I'm still undecided about that." He followed me out onto the steps, down into the dewy grass. The indigo sky still had a few reluctant stars studding it, but golden dawn welled in the east and brazed a few puffy clouds with fluorescent salmon. Everything here in the crater seemed hypersaturated with color, as if all filters were removed.

"What can I do to tip things in my favor?" I led him down the short path to the coffin-like box of the outhouse.

"I have to think on that."

That was not what I'd hoped to hear. I went into the outhouse, shut the door as best I could on the rope tied to my wrist. Sitting on the wooden seat, I was unable to pee, my bladder cramping.

A long moment passed.

"You done yet?"

"No. Sorry, I can't go." I got up, hoisted my pants, came out.

"Well, I have to go. Maybe that will help." He went inside, shut the door. I stood awkwardly, my hand with the rope on it extended to the door, looking around at the awesome vista. It occurred to me to untie the rope and try to run, but I had no confidence I'd make it more than a few yards before he caught me, and I felt like I'd tested his patience as far as I was willing to at the moment. Resigned, I soaked in the stark beauty and colors of the towering crater wall behind us, the sweep of the valley floor before us, the ocean in the way far distance, blue and mysterious, the sky given dimension by the brilliant clouds overhead.

I heard Russell Pruitt doing a very long pee, and suddenly I had to go in the strange way of these things, and as soon as he came out I darted in and did my business, number two as well. I came out carrying the folded squares of used napkin.

"Thanks for waiting," I said. "Gotta pack these out." Like I'd live to do that. I had to keep thinking like I would.

"Glad you could go. We might have been out here a long time," he said. "I want to fix us some breakfast; then we need to get on the trail to Holua Cabin."

He'd read the permits, after all.

The second time hope died was only slightly less painful than the first time.

Russell Pruitt locked us back into the cabin, untied the rope on my wrist. "You can pack your own things while I fix breakfast."

I thought of sassy things to say back, of trying to engage him in some discourse about the logic of taking me prisoner to do therapy, but in the end I just turned to my bunk and began packing up my meager belongings.

On the plus side of all of this, the physical misery of my

first days in the cabin was gone—and I couldn't chalk my rejuvenation up to just a dose of alcohol and a pasta dinner. The current peril I was in was having a salutary effect on my body—a side effect of the threat of death, I decided. This conundrum would be very interesting to do a sociological study on, if ever I could design one ethically. At that challenge, my overused brain boggled.

Rolling up my sleeping bag, the dirt and grass stains on the once-new fabric reminded me of the physical altercations of the day before. That reminded me of the butcher knife, still under the bunk across the room.

My situation would be greatly helped by the addition of a butcher knife.

Russell Pruitt banged a few pans in the sink, and I heard him filling the big pot with water. His back was turned. I let the flashlight I still carried in the leg of my sweats fall out, and I gave it a kick so that it rolled across the cabin under the same bed as the knife.

"Rats," I said loudly, glancing at him. He hadn't turned, but keeping him distracted and talking seemed a good idea. "You're good at cooking. Bet there's a story there."

"Yeah, actually there is." He turned back to the propane

grill with the big pot in one arm and the striker in the other. I walked deliberately across the room, got on my knees, and reached under the bed. The angle was out of his view unless he came around.

I really hoped he'd forgotten about the butcher knife.

"I always liked being in the kitchen. Guess you could say I had a knack for it. I'd cook for my foster families. Helped them like me, and thanks to my cooking, I had only three placements before the end of high school. What're you doing?"

The crack of suspicion in his voice made me jump, bumping my head on the bottom of the bunk. "My flashlight rolled under here." I shoved the butcher knife into my sleeve, moved it down against my side hoping I wouldn't cut myself, even as the fingers of my other hand curled around the slim, cool tube of the flashlight. "See?" I sat back up on my knees, held it up.

"Okay. Well, anyway, my first job out of high school was for a restaurant, as a sous-chef. But I'd already discovered I was even better at computers than food—and I bet you can guess which one pays more."

"You have to do what you love," I said, my heart thundering as I walked back to my backpack, wondering where I could hide a seven-inch butcher knife that he wouldn't see if he decided to check my bag again.

I turned the pack toward him and shoved the knife down into a slit where the straps attached to the stiff backing of the pack. The handle still protruded, so keeping all my movements rhythmic, I shook out the yoga pants, rolling them to wrap around the mouth of the backpack as if adding extra padding for the straps. "How did you switch from food to computers? And then to psychology?"

"I never went to school for computers. Just started fixing them for people, rigging up networks within houses, things like that. Began getting work under the table that way. When I had enough saved up, I got my own place, supported myself with my own little tech business. I was always going to school for psychology."

I felt a chill pass across my skin, a reminder of the crawlies of yesterday. That he'd majored in psych meant he'd invested a lot of time and effort into his revenge scheme, something that didn't bode well for me due to the foot-in-the-door principle—that is, the more little choices a person made in the direction of a certain course of action, no matter how bizarre or challenging it became, changing course became even harder because to do so meant admitting you'd been wrong hundreds of choices ago. The foot-in-the-door principle led to situations like the Jim Jones cult, where all voluntarily drank the Kool-Aid, though many were rational adults who knew what was happening and could have refused.

"So when did you start tracking my whereabouts?"

"Not that long ago, actually. When I met your son, Chris, at college."

I threw my head up to glare at him. I actually felt my eyes get hot as I said, "You leave him alone!"

"Oh my. Hit a nerve, there, did I?" He retrieved his back-pack, a vast dark green number the size of a sofa, and began filling it with the contents of the kitchen. "Quite the mama bear."

"Do what you want to me, but leave him alone," I whispered fiercely, feeling my hand steal under the yoga pants to curl around the plastic handle of the knife. The thought of Chris hurt brought on a vivid fantasy of stabbing Russell Pruitt, repeatedly, messily, and with no reservation. I panted with terror and anticipation, adrenaline flooding my system with the means to execute that fantasy.

"Don't worry," he said, his back invitingly exposed as he put the bag of pasta, coffee, and other foodstuffs into the depths of his pack. "I've got no beef with him. But it was meeting him that gave me the idea to track you, see what you were up to. I'd had a different plan up until then. But once I was observing you, I could see you were going downhill fast. I didn't want you to beat me to the bottom."

"Bottom," I repeated, releasing the handle of the knife, pushing it back down, sucking calming breaths to bring my heart rate down.

I'd just learned that I could easily murder someone who threatened my child. It was one thing to entertain that idea intellectually; it was another to come up against it baldly and with opportunity.

"Yeah, bottom. The end. Kicking the bucket. Tossing off this mortal coil. Pushing up daisies. Feeding the worms," he chanted.

"You know, Russell Pruitt, I don't think you really are dying," I said. The words burst out of my mouth and bounced into the room like bowling balls, disturbing our constructed universe. Words have power. Words define reality. And a new reality could change everything about our situation.

Now Russell Pruitt was the one to lift his head and glare, and his dark eyes were definitely less glassy than this morning.

"Yeah. I think you were told something that's some doc's best guess, but it's not true. Here you are, hiking Haleakala Crater, no small physical feat. Slinging a grown woman around in her sleeping bag. Eating pasta and shrimp, drinking vodka, and feeling better than you have in years. Yeah, I think this death diagnosis is bogus."

Somewhere in my intuition, I'd come up with an idea— an idea that, if I could infect him with it, would change everything. The idea was coupled with emotion: *hope that he would live*. And if he were going to live . . . I could live.

"No more talking," he said, and I knew the seed was planted. I shut my mouth and let it take root.

Chapter 14

*I*deas are viruses. They clamp on, drill through the epidural layer of denial and defenses, inject their DNA into the host cell, and then wait for baby viruses to be treacherously birthed. Good ideas are the ones that are hardest to shake and are the most compelling. The idea that Russell Pruitt might not be dying had timeless appeal.

No one wants to know he's dying. In fact, we're all wired to hate that idea very much.

I walked ahead of Russell Pruitt, the rope tied around my wrist, on the trail toward the far side of the bowl of the crater. According to the map, it was a traverse of four miles to Holua Cabin, and I could see most of it was going to be sand.

Russell Pruitt's ability to tolerate this hike would have a great deal to do with whether or not he allowed my offer of hope to take up mental residence; thus it behooved me to make sure he wasn't overexerting himself. Every five or ten minutes, as we headed back into the main crater well, I found a reason to stop. A rock in my shoe. Wheezing (not much acting needed) and dehydration. Mismatched back-pack strap length. Et cetera.

At each of these stops, I checked his color and how tired he seemed—and he was fine, a towering kid with Coke-bottle glasses and a backpack the size of Kansas who hadn't yet broken a sweat. Heart condition or not, he was twenty-something years old. I was the pushing fifty-year-old alcoholic divorcée who'd been drinking her meals and abusing Advil. My liver was probably shot to hell. I might be the one dying.

Bent over, trying to adjust my sock through the toe of my boot, it occurred to me that if I stressed him and he had one of his attacks, I'd be in a position to get away. I could just ditch my pack and run for it. Yeah, it wouldn't be pretty getting my butt out of the crater with no water, but with the consequences as dire as they were, I could get my hustle on and do it.

Suddenly it occurred to me that by infecting Russell Pruitt with hope, I'd done the same to myself. I'd cast the die in the direction of staying tied to his side like a not-very-happy mule on a trail ride, carrying a pack and a bad attitude.

That's the thing about ideas. They're free radicals, not controllable, and by trying to convince Russell Pruitt he could live, I'd "caught" that hope myself—one possible future that might well backfire. Caring that he lived, I might find myself unable to do what needed to be done—from untying myself to using the butcher knife whose handle was rubbing a blister on the back of my shoulder.

Thinking clearly about all the options was the way to stay in control, I decided, my eyes on the gray sand in front of me. I couldn't be overinvested in any one scenario of running away, disabling, killing, or even having Russell Pruitt walk out with me alive. I'd stay alert, and I'd take the path that offered the best chance of survival.

I'd have to know it when I saw it and be ready to act instantly.

The thought brought my heart rate up and sweat poured out of my pores, releasing that awful body odor born of booze and exertion. I straightened up, stopped, reached back for my water bottle.

"Thirsty."

"You look like hell," Russell Pruitt said. "Maybe you're the one dying."

I tipped back my head and laughed to hear my earlier thought so perfectly echoed, and he shook his head and strode by me. The rope yanked on my wrist, and I stumbled after him.

With Russell Pruitt setting the pace, we were definitely moving. Every time I tried to slow down, the rope yanked tight on my wrist, tugging me forward. I stumbled on at my top speed for a half hour at least. His heart seemed fine—it was mine that was overexerting. Finally, totally winded and facing a steep black-sand incline that wound up and around yet another multicolored cinder cone, I dug my heels in like the aforementioned mule. "Please. I need a break."

"All right."

Russell Pruitt steered us to the side of the path, where he helped me by lifting my pack and setting it on a boulder.

We'd eaten a breakfast he fixed at the cabin of oatmeal and boiled prunes that he'd spiced deliciously with cinnamon, but I was a little embarrassed to hear my stomach rumble loudly—and in another odd echo of our bodily functions, his belly rumbled too.

We grinned spontaneously—and Russell Pruitt opened his enormous pack. "I have a treat I've been saving for you."

He extracted a Tupperware container and opened it. Resting inside on a paper doily, shiny with glaze, plump with raisins, was a cinnamon roll.

Cinnamon rolls had been my favorite breakfast for twenty years, on a Sunday morning with Richard and Chris, drinking our coffee and reading the morning papers . . . I felt tears prickle my eyes as he handed me the Tupperware. I leaned over, putting my nose into the container, inhaling the sweet, sugary fragrance laden with memories.

"I can't believe you brought this."

"I was going to torture you with it," Russell Pruitt said, blinking rapidly behind his thick glasses. "I was going to get you really hungry and eat it in front of you, reminding you of your family and all you'd lost and would never see again. But I realized you're already starving, you're already grieving for all you've lost, and it just didn't seem fun anymore."

I couldn't take a bite of the cinnamon roll. I was crying too hard.

He took it out of my hands, put the top on and set it aside, and then he slung a huge arm around my shoulder and hauled me against his side. My head leaned on his chest, and I heard the thump and swish of his great big enlarged heart, and I cried some more onto his shirt.

He wasn't a psychopath. He cared about me, felt empathy for me.

"Is everything okay?" A tenor voice, concerned, unfamiliar. I opened my streaming eyes, peered through my unspeakable greasy hair, still clamped against Russell Pruitt's side.

Two male hikers stood in front of us. They wore matching Columbia hiking outfits, with sleek little backpacks and black hiking poles. Perfectly groomed, tanned, gleaming with health, they were as matched as a pair of Dobermans. I resented the intrusion and reminded myself I was supposed to be ready to act on my own behalf with agility and ruthlessness.

"My mom's grieving," Russell Pruitt said, his giant's

voice pitched low. "We've been scattering my dad's ashes on the trail all morning."

That's when I realized I'd succumbed to Stockholm syndrome.

Chapter 15

I kept my face against his shirt, the tears congealing on my cheeks at the ease and potency of his lie. Maybe he was a psychopath after all—how could he be so kind and yet such an agile liar? Which of the behaviors was being put on, or were they all?

"So sorry for your loss," one of the hikers said.

"That's a beautiful thing to do. Take care," echoed the other, and I felt the shift in Russell Pruitt's weight that told me he'd lifted a hand to wave to them.

I kept myself very still.

"They're gone." Russell Pruitt's voice really did have a texture to it, a heft like a complex fisherman's sweater, especially when heard through the barrel of his chest. I sat back up.

"I'll take that cinnamon roll now," I said, my voice cold. I brushed the tears off my cheeks. "You sure are a good liar."

"What was I supposed to say?" He snorted, but he sounded hurt. I told myself to remember how easily he'd lied when I met him at the door of the cabin. He was a bundle of contradictions: one moment sabotaging my sobriety by brute force, the next helping with my backpack. One moment cooking delicious oatmeal, the next tying me to him with a rope.

Russell Pruitt was so much more than he appeared to be.

He handed me the Tupperware, and I looked up the hill the hikers were doing at speed, watching their neat rear ends and glossy poles disappear over the top of the ridge. I would need my energy, now more than ever.

I ate the cinnamon roll in a few quick, hard bites, ignoring the explosion of flavor and the way the raisins burst against my tongue. I wouldn't have eaten it at all if I didn't need the energy, I told myself. I would be prepared to act on my own behalf with speed and ruthlessness. I didn't need to fall prey any longer to the emotional dependency pattern of

Stockholm, in which hostages and kidnap victims developed attachment to their captors.

"Let's get going," I said. I hoisted the pack and set off with renewed vigor.

"That sugar really gave you some juice," Russell Pruitt said after a long moment. "Wish I had one more for the hike out. I hear the Switchbacks Trail is pretty strenuous."

I didn't reply, preoccupied with the changes that had been subtly happening between us—the adjustment of our body rhythms to be in tune. The gradual shedding of layers of defense and pretense into self-disclosure. I'd accepted my captivity and stopped trying to run after being prevented a few times (albeit violently) and begun to have a motherly concern for Russell Pruitt's health.

His virus had infected me as effectively as mine had him.

I'd stopped noticing our surroundings, but as my frenzied thoughts wound to their sorry conclusion, I came back into my body and the mechanics of the hike. Weight on my tender back. Boots rubbing. Deep breathing as I did the hill as best I could, determined not to be yanked along behind my captor anymore.

Stockholm syndrome has to be confronted head-on with

facts, I told myself sternly, even as I considered telling Russell Pruitt that if he left me alone at the end of the hike, I would never tell anyone what had happened. I would even help find him medical and mental health support.

Then you'll have a crazy man with a fixation roaming around free to attack you or someone else. Constance's voice.

The fine-grained volcanic sand puffed up like breath with every step. The vivid streaks of color on the hill we were traversing were bright red, sienna, umber, mustard, and the red-purple of old blood. The sky above was a depthless, blind blue, unmarked by clouds.

I could hear Russell Pruitt panting behind me.

Good. I hope he drops dead.

Guilt stabbed me, but I pushed through it. Constance was right. Pruitt was not my son, my friend, or even my client. He was a kidnapper, a psychological torturer, a sick bastard who somehow blamed me for the ills of his own life. Russell Pruitt was my enemy.

And you better not forget it again, my dead twin concluded.

I felt angry, finally, and that gave me an additional burst

of energy. At the top of the hill, I stopped. It wasn't really a choice. I was tasting blood in the back of my throat. I bent over with my hands on my knees, looking back down the long gray trail, rainbow-colored cinder cone, and wide-open sky.

Fucking Maui, so distracting with its scenery, as if nightmares don't come true right here in the middle of beauty. Constance's voice was definitely getting louder.

Russell Pruitt had kept up with me, but it had cost him. He was pale, with greasy sweat sliding down his massive cheeks. "Wish I'd had a cinnamon roll too," he said with a flash of smile. His teeth were normal sized in his overlarge face, giving a fun-house-mirror effect.

I smiled back, because it was important that he think nothing had changed between us. We stood side by side, and I noticed how he copied my posture—a primary way to establish a connection with another person was to imitate their body language, and he'd been doing that since he ambushed me.

Russell Pruitt wasn't just good at cooking and hacking computers. He was damn good at psychology, too.

"Seems like you didn't like what I told those hikers,"

Pruitt said. "What would you like me to tell anyone else we meet?"

"The truth." I kept my voice soft, with a trace of humor.

"Ha. Good one." He seemed piqued, and turned and got a head start on the trail. My rope jerked tight and reminded me I was a prisoner.

I walked along behind him as we wound down into the central bowl of the crater. Mounds and formations created an undulating topography of lava in various states of degradation. The piercing sky blazed sun down on us, but wind whipped the warmth away before it could be felt, making the temperature perfect for hiking.

We passed a wooden barrier circling a deep hole marked DANGER. Mildly curious, I wished I could look into the pit, see into that deep lava tube. I wished yet again that I was alone, beginning to feel better from my acute withdrawals, that I was making this trek as I'd planned—a woman overcoming her past and her present.

Maybe that's what I was doing—only now I was doing it in the shadow of Russell Pruitt.

We entered a valley area with massed clouds ahead. This side of the crater was older. The cloud forest on the sides of

Haleakala had pushed uphill and crested into a broken rift of the volcano, moving into the crater and taming the raw lava by inches. From the trail, I could look down the valley formed by the disintegrated side of the volcano into jungle pouring all the way down to the far blue ocean.

I crushed a bit of native *pukiawe* shrub in my fingers, smelled its sharp, juniper-like scent. This area was being settled by plants and wildlife—grouse, lizards, and even a few red honeycreepers had come to sip the nectar of the bright yellow *mamane* blossoms blooming all around us.

"Let's take a break," Russell Pruitt said, hoisting his pack onto a boulder. I complied without speaking, resting my pack and then unstrapping myself from it, my wrist still tied.

I squatted behind the boulder and did what needed to be done, this time with no problems. His back to me, resting on the boulder, Pruitt had taken out a granola bar and his water jug; he ate and drank without offering me any. Something had definitely shifted between us.

I wasn't sure if it was to my benefit or not. I got out a snack too, and we ate in silence, our postures imitating each other, but as far apart as we could be and be tied together.

We started walking again, and Pruitt pointed to a side trail marked SILVERSWORD LOOP.

"Want to go through that?"

"Not really. It's up to you," I said.

He didn't reply, just put his head down and gave a tug on the rope. Apparently, he didn't want to see any more silverswords either; there were plenty on the main trail. We trudged on and, like before, I eventually got into a rhythm with him. Thoughts ceased and there was just the body moving, timeless and absorbing.

Holua Cabin appeared suddenly as we came around a knob of lichen-studded stone, identical to the other cabin and butted up against a grassy slope studded with boulders big as Easter Island heads. An emerald carpet of plushy grass rolled up to the front stoop, and a spigot leaked a few drops of crystalline water into a cement trough for a pair of nene in a reprise of my favorite aspects of the previous cabin. A picnic table in front completed the picture of rustic bliss.

"Get inside," Russell Pruitt said. "I have some things to do."

That didn't sound good. I went inside.

"Get into your sleeping bag," he ordered.

I took it out of my pack, unrolling it on a bunk identical to the one I'd left behind, and climbed inside, boots and all. I'd set the backpack beside me. I felt reassured by the handle of the butcher knife protruding up beside me, within reaching distance.

Russell Pruitt screwed the lock onto the inside of the door, went through the kitchen removing everything he thought I could use as a weapon, then went outside and locked me in from there.

He hadn't brought his backpack in, so I couldn't search it for my pepper spray. I heard him doing something out there, a rustling, and then silence as if he'd left.

"Russell Pruitt!" I called.

No answer.

Maybe he'd gone.

I had a few minutes to try to find something new that could change my situation—and the first thing I did was turn on my phone. Two bars lit up. It was a miracle. I hit Bruce's speed-dial button, the number a little worn from use, and was unable to speak when his familiar bass came on the line. "Caprice, how's rehab?"

"Oh my God," I stuttered. "I'm in the crater. I've been

taken prisoner by a giant. You have to help me!"

"What? Slow down, Caprice, you're talking crazy," Bruce said, and I looked up as I heard the rattle of the lock on the front door.

"Holua Cabin in Haleakala. I'm a prisoner. Help me!" I whispered fiercely. I turned the phone off and slid it into my pocket as the door flew open with such force it slammed against the wall, and the whole cabin shuddered.

The giant was back, and he was angry.

Chapter 16

W ho were you talking to?" he growled, filling the doorway and blocking the light.

"I was praying," I said. "I was asking God for help."

He stepped inside, turned, put the hasp and lock on. "I don't believe you. One thing I never found was a phone. You must have had it on you all this time."

"No. No phone on this trip. I was going low-tech."

"Dr. Wilson, for a psychologist, you're a lousy liar. Get out of the sleeping bag and turn out your pockets."

I promptly slipped the phone down alongside me and kicked it into the bottom of the bag. I felt it vibrating; Bruce was calling me back. Mercy of mercies, it was muted already. I got out of the sleeping bag, turned my pockets inside out.

"I know you had your phone with you; it's how I tracked you here," Russell Pruitt said, patting me down. His hands were clammy, and I noticed his color was bad again. I'd already made up my mind that if he had one of those spells, I wasn't going to get his nitro for him—and I wasn't going to do CPR. I was going to watch him die, if I ever got that lucky.

"I did have my phone, but I left it in the car. All part of the intervention I was doing with myself. The intervention that you interrupted."

He patted me down all the way to my shoes and then turned the sleeping bag upside down. The phone fell out with a *clunk*.

"You lied," Russell Pruitt said. "I think there should be consequences."

"Hm. So it's okay for you to lie to me, and to others in front of me, but I can't lie even in a situation where my life is in danger. I'd call that a double standard," I said.

Russell Pruitt hit Recent Calls and held up the phone. "Who is Bruce Ohale?"

"A guy I'm dating."

"Lies!" he bellowed, his face turning red. "All lies!"

He threw the phone on the ground and mashed it beneath his massive giant-boot. The phone crunched into shards and bits of what had been my lifeline: my video log, hundreds of pictures of Chris and my former life, and all the contact information of anyone who'd ever mattered to me—which of course, I'd never backed up.

I flung myself onto my bunk and burst into tears. "God damn you, Russell Pruitt! I hope you die and go straight to hell!"

Whatever he expected, it wasn't that, I could tell—but frankly, I wasn't in control, and all my attempts at strategy had backfired anyway.

"You lied," he repeated, and went into the kitchen. I heard him filling the big pot with water, unloading the backpack, turning on the stove, lighting a Pres-to-Log—all while I cried extravagantly into the sleeping bag.

Mood swings and excess of emotion are also part of detox. I'd definitely hit that stage.

Finally, he came to the door of the kitchen. I felt him looking down at me. "Stop crying," he said.

"I can't," I sobbed.

"It bothers me. Stop." Russell Pruitt sounded confused. Maybe he cared about me a little bit. The thought made me cry harder. He sat on my bunk, and it creaked in protest. He patted my back. "I know what you need. Some hair of the dog. Let me get you a drink."

"No! No means no, Russell Pruitt," I sobbed. "I'll never drink again, and you can't make me!" Which wasn't true, but I wanted it to be.

"Dr. Wilson. We're supposed to be doing my therapy. Please, stop crying." He sounded like Chris—I heard the echo of my son's voice begging me not to cry over his asshole of a father. I felt my son's strong young arms around me again, his hand patting my back.

But Russell Pruitt wasn't my son. It's part of Stockholm to relate to one's captor, I reminded myself, to ascribe positive characteristics to him like the kindness and love of my son. It was understandable but not acceptable.

I knuckled the tears out of my eyes. They were so puffy I could hardly open them, but I'd finally stopped crying.

Maybe Bruce would come to the cabin with the Maui Police Department and a troop of Park Service dudes in a helicopter. Maybe he wouldn't just think I'd been having the DTs in that incoherent message about the cabin and the giant.

"What should I fix for dinner?" I asked, standing up.

"Did you mean that about me dying and going to hell?" Russell Pruitt asked, following me into the kitchen.

"Of course not. I'm just upset." I needed to go back to keeping the giant happy. It had to be better as a strategy than pissing him off. I looked through the food on the counter. "I'd planned to do Top Ramen tonight. Will that be okay with you, if I dress it up with some other stuff?"

Russell Pruitt took the vodka bottle out of his bag. "Sure." He poured two plastic cups of it. Mine was much fuller. "I really think you need this, Dr. Wilson. I want you to be able to deal with what I'm going to tell you."

"You're going to tell me more?" I kept my back to him, my heart skipping a beat as my whole body twitched at the prospect of alcohol and new, unwelcome revelations. I took three packets of Top Ramen and ripped the ends open with trembling hands. I broke the corrugated noodles into the pot. "I want to fix some prunes too."

"I have some carrots in the cold bag," Russell Pruitt said.

"I'll cut those up."

He got them out and chopped them with a steak knife he'd produced. I prepared the prunes, laying them in the bottom of a bowl and pouring boiled water from one of our bottles over them.

"Remember I told you this was about justice? And you didn't see how it was justice that I came out here and found you?" he asked.

"Yes," I said cautiously.

He turned and held up the cup of vodka. It was sunshine-yellow plastic and shone like a beacon. "I really want you to drink this."

"I will, if you let me clean up what's left of my phone." Maybe the SIM card hadn't been destroyed. If I was going to bow to the inevitable, I wanted to get something in return.

"It's a deal," he said, and I took the cup. The vodka felt like acid as I took the first swallow, and while my body responded with the same joyous rhapsody as before, I felt those helpless tears start again.

I really, really didn't want to drink anymore.

I walked over to the smashed phone, knelt. The main body of the sturdy early version iPhone was bent and mangled, rays of broken plastic forming a starburst pattern in the center of the rectangle of metal. Bits had spread from where he'd kicked them. I took another sip of vodka and looked at the mess.

"We need something to put this trash in."

"Use the plastic from the Top Ramen."

I went back into the kitchen, took one of the bags, knelt, and began putting broken glass, plastic, and metal parts into the crinkly plastic.

"So here's why I picked you for my therapy." Russell Pruitt leaned in the doorframe of the kitchen, looming over me. "My mother was killed by my dad. Domestic violence, you know. And then you evaluated my father. Testified against him for the prosecution. He had consecutive life sentences. He didn't make it past a year."

"Oh no." I sat back on my heels, looking at him. My eyes stretched, filling. "Oh no. Russell Pruitt, are you Hank Gardo's son?"

"The very same," he said. "I changed my name after the case." And I knew I was in very deep trouble indeed.

I threw back the rest of the vodka in a couple of big, hard swallows.

On my hands and knees, I kept picking up phone bits, the alcohol lighting a fire in my stomach. My fingers closed around the main metal case. I sat up and twisted it, and a shower of innards and shards fell out, along with the small metal piece that was the SIM card. It was still in the frame that had once been a loading slot. I slid it into my pocket and put the rest of the phone into the Top Ramen bag, thinking about Hank Gardo.

Hank was a psychopath of the successful white-collar type. He had been implicated in the disappearance of several women in his downtown Honolulu building. Honolulu Police Department had brought me in to watch footage of his interviews and to review his case file, and I'd identified him as one of those truly horrible human beings with something missing in his brain that drove him to seek thrills at the expense of others.

Three female temp clerks had disappeared before Gardo tipped his hand by beating and strangling his wife.

I remembered testifying and spotting a tall teenager with thick glasses sitting next to some sort of caregiver midcourt as I talked about the mind-set of the man who'd been habitually abusing his wife and one day had simply gone too far as his hunger for violence escalated. I remembered looking at that dark-haired kid and hoping he had somewhere to go.

We hadn't been able to get Hank Gardo for the temp clerks—but we'd been able to work the sentencing so he got consecutive life sentences, and six months into his bid, he'd died at the hands of another inmate. I'd felt a sense of relief at the time.

"You're awfully quiet," Russell Pruitt said.

"I was remembering you in the courtroom at your father's trial," I said, getting up to walk to the corner where an old corn-stick broom rested. I swept the area and scooped the last shards of my lifeline into the dustpan, kneeling on the floor. "Why did you change your name?"

"For obvious reasons." He leaned on the doorway of the kitchen, stirring the Top Ramen in the pot with a wooden spoon. "I remember you too."

"I did my job, Russell. I assessed your father as a Psychopathic Disorder with co-occurring Narcissistic Personality Disorder—yes, I'm using that diagnosis a little early before the DSM-Five makes it official. Hank was a very violent man. We couldn't get him for the temp clerks that disappeared from his building—but he slipped up by killing your mother."

"It was a bad time for me." Russell Pruitt stirred the noodles. A shock of his thick, greasy hair shielded his eyes, and his massive shoulders were hunched.

I came closer, made eye contact with him. Behind those thick lenses, his eyes had that glassy look again, his cheeks pale. Perhaps his heart was stressed—I wanted to hope so but couldn't bring myself to. I felt sick with compassion for all he'd been through. "I'm so sorry. I remember hoping you had somewhere loving to go."

"Turns out I didn't. And I don't want your pity. It's your fault my dad got the sentence he did." His voice was a low growl.

"Think about it. I did my job. I work for the state, and I get the cases they give me. If it hadn't been me, it would have been another psychologist."

"But it was you." He tapped the spoon on the edge of the pot. "My gigantism began during the trial. The pediatrician said the stress might have thrown my pituitary gland out of whack."

I walked back, knelt on the floor, brushing the bits of broken phone into the dustpan. It seemed the safest place at the

moment. It was important not to argue with him; my desire
to defend myself would only activate the intermittent rage
I'd already experienced.

"It must have been terrible."

"It was. As I grew, I kept thinking that if my dad hadn't
died, I might have had somewhere to go—but even I knew
he was scary, and I didn't really want to live with him. So
I wanted to understand him, and my mom, and why she
stayed with him. And I wanted to find out if psychopathy is
inherited."

I breathed slowly, quietly, on my knees. "And what did
you learn about that?"

"There seem to be two kinds of psychopathy—those that
arise from environmental factors and those that have a ge-
netic brain chemistry component."

"That's right. It seems like you're really wondering about
yourself. The developmental task of the adolescent and
young adult is identity formation—discovery of who, what,
and how you are in the world."

"That's what I came to find out." Russell Pruitt's eyes
blinked rapidly behind the glasses as he turned to look at
me. "What do you think, Dr. Wilson? Am I a psychopath?"

Chapter 17

*D*on't tell him he's a psychopath! Constance shrieked in my mind. *This isn't real therapy—remember, keep the giant happy!*

"I don't know," I said. It was the truth.

"C'mon, Dr. Wilson. That's a cop-out."

"Asking me is a cop-out. I can't give an honest answer; my life is at stake. So that should give you something to consider."

A long silence stretched out between us.

"Fair enough." He stirred the Top Ramen. "We'll talk more about this. Dinner's ready."

I got up off my knees and walked into the kitchen,

dumped the last bits from the dustpan into the trash. "I don't know how much you're aware of regarding the diagnostic process. What classes have you had so far?"

"Got the basics in my bachelor's. Next semester I've got Theories of Personality, Abnormal Psychology, Social Psychology Methods, and Overview of the DSM."

"Those are the theoretical basics. Applied assessment and interviewing is a lot of practice experience that you'll get in your internship." I washed my hands under the cold, cold water piped straight out of the aquifer in the heart of the volcano. "Any diagnostic impression of you would be complicated by the severe trauma you went through in witnessing the domestic violence between your parents. Your gigantism is another aspect that makes your mental health profile complicated—impaired pituitary function can lead to impulse control problems."

"I'm actually more of a planner than impulsive."

"I agree, given how you set up this situation, but personally, I think character isn't ever preformed or inherited."

"Character," Russell Pruitt said. "That's not a word you hear very often anymore."

"What I mean by character is the sum total of acted-out,

observable behavior. Character has fallen out of fashion, but it's still a great way to think about who you want to be in life. You know that old saying—sow a thought, reap an action. Sow an action, reap a habit. Sow a habit, reap a character. Sow a character and reap a destiny. What we do here in this cabin, in the time we have left to us, is the fruit of our character and becomes our destiny."

"Very poetic." Russell Pruitt drained the noodles in the sink beside me, using the lid to keep them in the pot. Steam rose and wreathed his glasses. "I think it's an experiment."

"Hmm. Tell me more." I spooned the prunes into two chipped china cups and carried them to the table. He followed me, carrying bowls of the noodles and a couple of metal forks.

"It's an experiment as to whether or not I have the same capacity for violence as my father. Is the revenge I've planned something I have to act on, or something I can resolve some other way?" Russell slurped some hot noodles, his eyes still hidden by fogged lenses.

"Right. Good questions." I blew on the hot noodles, my heart thudding and stomach churning. The topic was utterly unnerving, but as long as I treated it as a source of intellectual inquiry, I could engage him in a dance of words that might somehow set me free. "I'd like to make a case that you are not a psychopath."

"I bet you would," he said, and smiled that funhouse grin.

I persevered. "Certainly you have trauma. Unresolved parent issues. An obsessive quality even. Narcissism and a problem with anger and impulse control. But I'm not convinced that you're a psychopath."

"Why not?" His voice sounded deep, hopeful, young—a Stradivarius of a voice that could adopt shades of meaning. I reminded myself not to trust that naive tone—he'd fooled me with it before.

"Well, you've been kind to me, and even when you laid hands on me, it was not to inflict pain that you then enjoyed. It was because you were angry or to make a point. There was a function to it."

You're making excuses for him, Constance whispered. *Please tell me you don't really believe that crap.*

"I've been kind, yes. I didn't have to bring you a cinnamon roll and let you eat it."

"Right. You seem to be upset when I'm upset. That implies a level of empathy, and a lack of empathy, or inability to feel others' emotions, is one of the primary hallmarks of the psychopath."

Russell Pruitt seemed to be thinking this over. "So you don't think I can kill you, then?"

"Oh no. I think you can kill me, all right." I turned my blue eyes on him. "I just think you'll regret it forever if you do."

I've been told my eyes are very effective at seeing the depths of clients—and the depths I saw in Russell Pruitt were confused. Confusion I could handle.

"I think you'll be sorry if you kill me and will never feel right about it." I pitched my voice low, with the cadence of a hypnotic suggestion. "You don't want to kill me."

I drove that suggestion deep. His eyes showed the telltale circle of white beneath the iris that confirmed he was under hypnosis. "You want to live. You want me to live too."

"I want to live," Pruitt repeated. "I want you to live." Then he shook his head like a bear with a mosquito in its ear. "Enough of this. The noodles are getting cold."

After our meal, he said, "I want to keep going with our therapy, but we're going outside. Let's each get some logs."

I walked into the storage closet, identical to the one at the other cabin, and loaded my arms with four of the Pres-to-Logs in their brightly marked paper packaging. Pruitt was waiting in the doorway with the rope in his hands, and I rolled my eyes.

"Oh, come on. Do you really think I'm going to run off? With no water? And night coming on?"

Russell Pruitt held up the rope, considering.

"Okay. You can take off your boots. I don't think you'll run off without your boots. Or, you can be tied."

Holding the Pres-to-Logs, I considered. "I think that's an unfair choice. You still don't trust me."

"Of course not. Choose."

"Okay then. I don't like the way the rope makes me feel. I'll do without the boots."

"Socks too," he said. I went to the bed, set the logs down, untied the boots.

I'd left them on without taking them off for two days now. My feet reeked, and they were reddened and sore from hiking, the skin blanched from sweat and blistered on the tops of my toes. Taking the boots off and rubbing my feet with the dirty socks, I was surprised at the sense of freedom my bare feet gave me.

Maybe this was going to be my chance. I glanced up at the windows—another glorious sunset was flaming in the crater, and it would be full dark soon. But I still had the flashlight and striker bulb down in the leg of my elastic-bottomed sweatpants, and something Russell Pruitt didn't know was that I loved being barefoot. I did all my yard work barefoot. Like many Hawaii residents, I had tough soles on my feet from wearing slippers or nothing on the weekends, and I thought I might be able to do the trail bare-foot . . . The thought of the lacy-sharp edges of the pum-ice I'd picked up earlier intimidated me, but I'd cross that bridge when and if I came to it.

He'd offered me a choice, and I chose the option that seemed to give me the most likely chance for escape.

Now, if I could just get a few other things . . . "I'd like to get my jacket on if we're going outside."

"Definitely." He went to his own backpack and dug through it. I turned to mine and considered the butcher knife.

I discarded the idea of carrying it. It was just too big to conceal, and the possibility of cutting myself too real. I needed some water, though, and my car keys if I ever did get my chance.

I pulled out my nylon jacket with its zippered pockets and, at the same time, felt the side pocket of my backpack. He'd taken the car keys. Another tiny blow, eating away at my resolve. Still, all I had to do was get out of the crater alive, and I could wave someone down.

I zipped up the nylon jacket and picked up a full water bottle. "Okay."

Russell Pruitt picked up his own load of Pres-to-Logs. "Follow me."

I felt dizzy with the liberty of following him untethered outside the cabin. Farther to the west than Kapala`oa Cabin, Holua's sunset view was completely blocked by the huge cliff behind us, the western wall of the crater. All I could see of the sunset was a row of clouds marching along the jagged edge of the rim, stained crimson and gold.

Standing on the plushy green grass, though chilly, felt great on my feet, and I wriggled my toes, looking down the valley. "I wonder where the trail out is."

Pruitt pointed with one of his sausage fingers to the east. "See that headland? Switchbacks go all the way up that."

My heart sank.

The way out was going to be at least as strenuous as the way in. The headland looked to be a couple of miles away across rugged lava on the floor of the crater. Even from where I stood, I could see the trail was steep and all uphill, climbing the impressively steep wall of the crater by winding back and forth. I remembered it was a total of four miles on the map—technically not that long, but at an elevation of ten thousand feet, nothing to sneeze at.

"Come with me." He walked around the back of the cabin.

I followed him, carrying the logs and my water bottle on top of them. A narrow trail led straight up the cliff directly behind the cabin, and we navigated that carefully. As soon as I was off the grass and on the trail, I discarded the idea of running away without my boots. The dirt was soft enough, but it was punctuated by knurls of raw lava, poky as stone burrs. I found myself slowing down, mincing, trying not to step on the painful stones as Russell Pruitt headed for a dark opening in the cliff face.

"Where are we going?" I asked.

He didn't answer.

This must have been where he was when I was making my call to Bruce.

God, please help Bruce find me, I prayed, as I stepped onto the rough, chill stones lining the floor of the cave. *Please. Soon.*

Russell Pruitt had turned on his flashlight. The inside of the cave, a tall, narrow space with bench-like stones lining the walls, had been the scene of various kinds of revelry in the past—Tibetan prayer flags decorated one wall, empty liquor bottles another, and stubs of colored candles had been stuck into the stone, one melted onto the next.

"Seems like people party in here," I said, wrinkling my nose against a smell of stale urine.

"Yeah. Thought we could talk in here this evening. Let's make a fire."

"I'm sure the Park Service wouldn't like that."

"The Park Service wouldn't like a lot of things about what we're doing." Russell Pruitt took three of the logs, made a little tepee of them, and lit them. Flames licked up the paper wrappers and into the air in a spiral of smoke that made me squint.

I sat on one of the stone "benches" near the opening. I imagined making a run for it, powering down the trail on my once-muscular legs and tender feet, past the cabin, through the razor-like lava field and then into the dark up the Switchbacks Trail.

Even if I could outrun Russell Pruitt without my boots, which was highly unlikely, getting far enough ahead of him to actually escape seemed impossible. I needed my boots and a good long head start. I'd seen what Russell Pruitt could do, and he was at least as good a hiker as me even with his heart condition.

"So. We're going to share our stories. Get some accountability." The flare of the Pres-to-Logs danced across Russell Pruitt's face. I realized his features reminded me of the way a face drawn on a balloon is distorted when you blow it up. Not pretty, and not his fault. I felt that compassion again—poor, sick, suffering boy.

He could have just gone to counseling, Constance said. *He didn't have to stalk you and take you captive.*

"You go first," I said. "I want to hear what you have in mind."

"Okay. So. I told you already that when I started out

to find you, I wanted to hurt you, and make you witness my pain and feel it too."

I didn't know how to respond. I suppressed the lurch of my heart and just listened, keeping my neutral psychologist face on.

"Well, that's changed as I've gotten to know you. I now want us both to get something out of this experience, some sort of healing. I still want to do therapy with you, but now I want to help you with yours. I've begun some internship hours, you know. I'm working at a crisis shelter for teens. I talk to all kinds of runaways, abuse victims."

"Sounds like a perfect fit for you." I wondered how genuine all this was, this change of inclusion from "me" to "us." He could be becoming attached to me, and that meant he might not kill me. The firelight flickered on those thick glasses, making his eyes impossible to see.

"Yeah. Well, to start with, my dad wasn't always terrible at home."

"They seldom are."

"I remember my parents being happy. When I was younger. But as I got older, he'd come home late from work.

When he came home late, it was a bad night. Mom would have me lock my door. She bought me a CD player that spun stars across the ceiling of my room and played songs through headphones. I turned it on as loud as it would go, but it was never loud enough to drown out the sound of them fighting, of him beating her."

"That's very hard on a child."

"Yes. I wanted to help her, but I was scared of him too. I think on some level I knew he just wasn't like other people. It took me until I was thirteen to realize he didn't love me, never had, and all the hugs and Christmas gifts and baseball games—they were only so people thought we were normal. I was a prop in the 'home and family' set piece." Russell Pruitt had begun panting shallowly, the flickering light dancing patterns on his sweating face. "In the morning after a bad night, Mom would be in bed with a 'migraine.' Dad would fix my breakfast on those days, always extra cheerful. I remember how he'd make me pancakes with blueberries in them. Only on the days she had migraines."

"You realized your parents were both participating in the masquerade." I summarized the content of his story. Doing so helped keep me disengaged from the heartbreaking threads of it. "Your mom came up with a health complaint she could use to disguise the beatings. You were scared and felt trapped and conflicted."

"Yes, that's it exactly." He ran his hands through his thick black hair, looked into the flames. "I didn't know anything about the other people he might have killed until the trial, when I read the papers. The allegations about the other women who disappeared and how many times he was questioned—it made me feel sick inside. His sickness was in me, like his DNA was warped—and had warped me."

"You found a reason for your gigantism."

He looked at me, a long pause. The flames reflected in those thick Coke-bottle lenses, a spooky effect.

"You're very good, Dr. Wilson. I can see I have a long way to go as a therapist before I'm as good at getting to the heart of things as you are."

I didn't reply.

Silence is also a powerful tool in therapy. He was naming a future for himself, a future that wasn't yet hopeless but would never happen if he killed me. I had to let that work its own powerful magic on him—its infection of hope.

Russell Pruitt having hope was going to keep me alive. I still wasn't sure myself if he was too far gone to be salvaged, to be healed, and even to have a future in psychology someday. I'd always believed in change and second chances—I wouldn't have a career in this field if I didn't—but at this point, all that swirled around us were possibilities and dust.

"The day he killed my mother was kind of like all the rest. That's what stands out to me—that I didn't realize it was going to be different." Pruitt leaned forward toward the warmth of the flames, which were taking a while to warm the small cavern. The smoke was escaping somehow—there must be a vent in the ceiling. I wished I'd worn my boots after all, and tucked my feet up to keep them warm, wrapping my arms around my knees.

"I did my homework after dinner, thinking he was going to be home late, and that wasn't good—usually he'd go out drinking, or as I later read, stalking his prey—and he'd come home boozed up with that need to start something with Mom. But he'd been better lately. It didn't always end that way, so I was hopeful. Now I know that's intermittent reinforcement—when something doesn't *always* happen a certain way. You get hopeful something might be different."

I waited, hoping he wouldn't get to thinking about hope and what an infection it could be. Hoping he'd tell the story and that it would give him some relief—and at the same time, wishing I didn't have to hear it. I knew how it ended. I'd been a witness at the trial.

"So I did my homework. Mom helped me with the math. I could tell she was worried and nervous—she kept looking at the clock and cleaning everything even though it was perfect, because how she kept the house was something he'd pick on, or if she didn't look pretty enough. Mom was always pretty."

I sighed, remembering his mother's picture. She'd been an old-fashioned kind of beautiful, with a sweet oval face, olive skin, and curly black hair. She'd been average height, with a nice slim figure. She wasn't the "type" he'd disappeared—they were chubby, dyed blondes. No one, including me, had been able to figure out what he had against chubby dyed blondes, and Hank Gardo had never said.

"She made me take my shower and go to bed early. I was in bed, listening to music, and hoping it would be okay when he got home. But it wasn't. It started like it always did, with some accusation and her trying to appease him— and it escalated. I heard them running around and her trying not to scream because she didn't like to scare me. And I put my pillow over my head and shut my eyes. I fell asleep."

"You're still mad at yourself. You wish you hadn't shut it out. You wish you'd done something." I named his unspoken guilt.

"Yes." He breathed a long sigh of relief to be so understood. Firelight caught the tears falling off his chin. This was the gift of witnessing his story. It was all I could give him. "When I woke up, it was over. He'd gone, and he'd left her there."

I remembered the crime scene photos. I wished I didn't.

"I came out. She was in the kitchen, on her back. He'd beaten her so much that I couldn't recognize her face. She didn't get up, and she didn't move."

"It's a terrible thing that happened to you both."

"I called nine-one-one, and I didn't touch her because I

watched *CSI* even though I wasn't supposed to, and I knew not to touch her."

"You were smart and brave. You did everything right." I knew I was talking to a kid right now, a traumatized child evident in the high pitch and rapid cadence of his deep voice.

"I sat in the doorway. I prayed they would get my dad, that they would shoot him dead. When the cops came, they asked if I'd touched anything, and I said no."

"You did all you could. Smart and brave boy."

"I just sat there in the doorway and looked at the kitchen. There was a broken pane with blood on it in the glass dish cabinet. I thought he must have thrown her into it. The dinner she'd made him was all over the floor. It was meat loaf, mashed potato, and green beans, and the meat loaf was stuck on the wall above the sink. The plate had broken all over where he threw it and she had mashed potato in her hair."

"You noticed a lot of details and you remember them clearly even though you were in shock."

"Was I in shock? I thought I must be like him, because I

didn't feel anything. I didn't cry. I just looked around and tried to remember everything so I could help with the case."

"You were—what? Twelve? You lived in a world where you'd always been braced for this. You couldn't afford to feel anything, and you did the best you could to help your mother."

"I like that better than what I've been thinking about myself." Russell Pruitt darted me another swift glance, and I reached over and set my hand on his shoulder. It was the first time I'd voluntarily touched him. "A social worker came. She took me to a foster family. They were nice, but I didn't talk. I couldn't talk to anyone but the cops. They finally had me talk to the police psychologist."

"Someone like me."

"I guess."

"You didn't want to trust anyone. You didn't want to care or attach to anyone. It's a natural response to the kind of trauma you'd been through."

"Yes." He looked at me, a quick glance. "You understand."

"I do."

"The prosecuting attorney got a psychologist in to work with me, get me ready for the trial—because they'd picked him up that very morning. He'd just gone to his favorite bar, in his dirty shirt and with bloody fists, and waited for them to come get him."

"He'd gone too far. He knew there was nowhere to run."

"I guess so." Russell Pruitt turned his enormous hands over. Gilded by firelight, they almost looked graceful. He turned them back and forth. "I started growing during the trial."

"And you explained what happened to yourself as internalizing his distortion."

"Right. But now I'm wondering."

"That's what this trip has been about. Discovering what is you and what is him."

Russell Pruitt nodded. I took my hand off his shoulder and put it in my lap, feeling a bone-deep sadness as I did so. Still, objectivity was good practice, and in this situation, really hard to come by. Russell Pruitt had worked his gigantic, brokenhearted magic on me, and I cared about him now. It was no good denying it. I needed to stay alive so I could help us both."

"Your turn," Russell Pruitt said.

I shook my head. "No. It's not about me. It's about you."

He took his glasses off, wiped them on his T-shirt. His dark brown eyes were normal sized, long-lashed. I imagined his mother's eyes had been much like his, since Hank Gardo had had gray eyes. "It's not just about me. You came on this journey to settle some things for yourself, to figure some things out—to get sober. I interrupted all that, and I want you to get what you came here for."

"It sounds like you've decided to let me live," I said carefully, repeating the suggestion I'd given him earlier.

He put the glasses back on. "I want to. But I can't figure a way out of the situation we're in. So how about we not deal with that tonight, and you tell me your story."

I sighed, settled back against the bumpy stone wall, tucking my feet under me as best I could.

"Telling my story seems irrelevant when tomorrow I might die. I just don't see a point. Makes it hard for me to do anything but worry about self-preservation. This is why coercion of any kind is counterproductive to therapy."

Russell Pruitt considered this, rubbing his chin with the tips of his fingers. "I honestly don't want to kill you. But how can I let you live?"

"We have several options. Why don't we talk about them and then you can think about them tonight?" I held my breath, hoping he'd go along.

In the meantime, maybe Bruce will find us, Constance said.

"Okay. I'm interested in what you've come up with." Pruitt moved a log farther into the fire.

"Good. Okay, the first, and easiest, is that I don't say anything to anybody about what has happened here. We hike out and go our separate ways."

"Provided I accept your promise that you won't tell."

"True. Second, we walk out together and you turn yourself in. I help you get the proper support for your health. That's my favorite option."

"I'd have to be willing to submit to the system, and that's a big *if.* Watching my dad's trial and being a foster kid didn't exactly encourage me to throw myself into the arms of blind justice."

"Okay. Third, you can tie me up and leave me in the cabin. Escape, take all my money, et cetera, and make a run for it."

"This scenario has possibilities, but you have too many connections. I think law enforcement would be trying very hard to find anyone who'd laid a hand on their psychologist. I'd have to start a whole new life, and I like the life I have going on."

The Pres-to-Logs were burning down. Russell Pruitt got up and piled on the ones I'd brought, and the paper-covered tepee flared up again. I noticed the inks flamed different colors: green, red, and blue.

"Well, that brings up one last point I want you to think about. If you kill me, they're going to be much more on your case, and you've left a ton of trace in both cabins, all over my things. If you kill me, don't you think the stakes will be that much higher for your capture? And how will you be able to resume your old life? The statute of limitations runs out on terroristic threatening and kidnapping, which is the most you'll face now—but there's no statute of limitations for murder."

Russell Pruitt rubbed his hands together. They made a dry, whisking noise that raised the hairs on my arms, and I wondered if I'd gone too far toward popping his bubble of denial. I decided to switch gears. "I've been wondering about the shoe."

Chapter 18

*T*he shoe?" He slanted a dark eye at me. He really did have some lovely long eyelashes. I swear I could see Ruth Gardo looking out of her son's eyes. Maybe Ruth's spirit would win over Hank's—a fanciful notion.

"The shoe. Cream-colored pump, size eight, mud all over it."

"Oh, that." Russell Pruitt smiled. "I thought that would get to you. It's Angie Pinheiro's. Poor girl had to be a bridesmaid again a few weeks ago. I didn't think she'd miss it."

"Angie." I covered my mouth with my hand. "She's always had such bad luck."

"Yeah, no kidding. Struck by lightning? Broke her back horseback riding? Finally gets married, and he's a bigamist and a gambler?" Russell Pruitt shook his big shaggy head. "She's cute though. I thought of asking her out, being her fourth strike of bad luck."

"Thanks for not asking her out. She'd go, you know. She has no sense of personal safety."

"So you don't think I'm safe."

"Not really, no. Weren't we just discussing whether or not you were going to kill me?" Incredibly, we looked at each other and laughed. I smacked my knee. "You and Angie. What a pair, damn!"

"Hey," Pruitt said. "You should take this more seriously."

"Why? Taking it seriously just makes me sad about things I can't change. I love Angie. I care about her, and I feel bad for her. Thinking of you breaking into her closet and stealing her dirty bridesmaid shoe—it's just so sad, Russell Pruitt, that it's funny." I laughed some more, and there was definitely an edge of hysteria in my voice.

Russell Pruitt shifted. "You still haven't told your story."

"I still don't see the point."

"You could work some personal issues out. I could help you figure out what's next for you."

"Hard to care when I don't know if I'll live past tomorrow."

"Okay, I promise I won't kill you tomorrow. Does that help?"

"Weird, but it kind of does." I extended my hands to the fire. Unlike Russell Pruitt's, my fingers were almost transparent, the skin pale and waxy. With the fire behind them, I could see the glowing red outlines of my slender bones. "Okay. I'll talk about something you might be able to help me with. You see, my husband ran off with a woman."

"I know."

"Yes, you do. Anyway, Chris is at school, and Richard is gone, and frankly, I don't want him back. One thing I discovered recently is that I hadn't loved him for a long time. I'd just been in the habit of thinking I did. Well, I kept the house to hold on to something of the life I had before, and now it's not feeling good. It just reminds me of what I've lost." I twisted my fingers together, feeling the loss of my wedding band. I'd taken it off six months ago, and my finger still felt funny. "It's part of why I drink. To fill the house with sound, to not feel so alone. I think, as part of my sobriety, I need to move."

"Sounds like you do."

"Yeah. I've always wanted to live by the ocean, but it was too expensive. Well, it's not too expensive to get an ocean-front condo for one, just a little studio."

"Good idea."

"So that's why I think this talk is a waste of time. It assumes I've got a future to figure out. And anyway, Hector wouldn't like it."

"He'd get used to it."

"You know about Hector?"

"I know everything about you."

"Really?"

"Well, not everything." Russell Pruitt stood, dusted his pants. "I have been studying you for a while, though."

"God. I am so boring." The floor of the cavern felt cold and gritty to my bare feet as I got up. "I can't imagine how that was any fun."

Russell Pruitt looked around for something to bank the

fire and ended up dropping rocks on it. Sparks flew up in swirls as we withdrew to the entrance of the cave. "I'm kind of glad the surveillance stage is over. It was hard to stay mad at you once I saw what your life was like."

"Great. That's just grand." I followed him, walking tentatively, out into the star-spangled vault that was the crater, the air breathlessly cold. He shone the flash on the rocky trail, and we made slow progress to the cabin after a pit stop at the outhouse. Once there, he locked us in.

We brushed our teeth in companionable silence, and I washed my sore, dirty feet with a rag from the sink and put my socks back on. He turned off the lamp after I was back in my sleeping bag, and sheltering darkness surrounded us.

"Good night, Dr. Wilson."

"Call me Caprice."

"Good night, Caprice. That's such a funny name for a psychologist."

"I'm aware."

"What's the story behind it?"

I wriggled a bit in my sleeping bag. The dark of the cabin seemed to invite secrets, and he knew so many anyway.

"My mom was fanciful. I had a twin. Her name was Constance."

"Constance and Caprice. A twin?"

"Yes. She died when we were fourteen."

"I didn't know that." Pruitt sounded irritated.

"I'm surprised you didn't turn that up. It was quite the drama at the time." I kept my voice light.

"I was focusing on the more recent past. Cute names."

"It might have been cute, but I always thought it was more ironic. A misnomer. I was the steady, dependable one, and Constance the impulsive one. She ran out in the road and was hit by a car." Old pain, like that of a phantom limb, stole my breath. "I still miss her. She shouldn't have died."

"That's heavy," Russell Pruitt said. We fell silent.

He'd promised me another day, and maybe Bruce would come. I had to live so Constance, my mirror image, my identical set of DNA, could live too. I eventually drifted into dreams, and Constance was with me, laughing and running.

She was always laughing and running in my dreams.

Chapter 19

I woke up to Russell Pruitt's giant hand smothering me. My eyes flew open to see his bulk beside me, a shadow like a mountain, and the hand was heavy as a side of beef, cutting off all air. I clawed at his wrist, and he moved the hand down so my nostrils were clear. Squatted down beside my bed, he held a finger up to his lips so my bulging eyes could see he meant me to be quiet. Outside the cabin, I heard voices.

"Do you think anyone's in there?" A loud woman's voice.

"Don't know. It looks locked up." I heard the voices moving around outside, discussing whether they had time to boil water and refill their water bottles. I pictured them, these unknown and cheerfully loud hikers, sitting at the picnic table, taking pictures of the nene, haggling over the granola bar— having no idea of the tense situation in the nearby cabin.

"Let's not boil water. We're supposed to be in Kapala'oa Cabin, and since we got down here so early, I'd like to make it there before it gets too hot," the male hiker said.

Russell Pruitt's hand covered most of my face. With a movement a few centimeters to the right, he'd be able to smother me with so little effort it made my heart flutter, an overworked hummingbird. I longed to remind him he'd promised me another day, but his head was turned toward the door as he knelt beside my bunk.

So I lay there and endured my helplessness until the hikers finished their snack and we heard their voices fade.

"They're gone." Pruitt took his hand away from my face.

I batted at it reflexively as I sat up. "That was a very scary way to wake up."

"I'm sorry. I didn't know what you would do."

"We're right where we were before. There's no useful process without trust." I swung my legs to the side, sat up, and went to the kitchen sink. I splashed the very cold clear water on my hands and face. There were tears on my cheeks, and I hadn't even felt them falling. I stopped myself from mindlessly gulping the untreated water and picked up one of the water bottles, drinking half of it down.

"Not true. We have a day together and we haven't decided what we're doing. I got up early and found a trail back behind the cabin. I thought we could go explore a little bit, stretch our legs."

"Okay. Whatever you want—you're the boss." I felt listless and exhausted after the surge of panic and remembered I was still having withdrawals. I went back to the bunk, lay down.

"I'll fix some breakfast; then we'll go." He busied himself in the kitchen.

I didn't answer. I was thinking about Constance. I was all we both had left. I'd always had everything inside me that Constance did. Everything, including the steely resolve to have her way. And I could feel how powerfully she wanted two things—for me to live and for me to get sober.

I became a psychologist to understand better what it had all been about. Her. Me. Her death. What it did to our family. This was my story—the story I saw no point in telling Russell Pruitt, who was stirring oatmeal on the stove.

He doesn't deserve to know our story, Constance said. *Don't fall for his mind games.*

A scent of cinnamon with a chaser of prunes filled the air like a solid, tasty substance. My stomach rumbled in response.

"You're awfully quiet," he said.

I shut my eyes and pretended to be asleep.

"People say twins can communicate mentally sometimes. Did you and Constance do that?"

I didn't answer even as I heard Constance chuckle in the back of my mind. I wished I'd never said anything to him about my twin, let him that far into my head. Lying on my bunk, gathering my energy, I had an insight.

Russell Pruitt was never going to just walk away and leave me alone. Even if he didn't kill me, it wouldn't be enough to just escape. I had to get him locked up, get him psychiatric help. There was no other way this could end, because he already knew so much about me, and chances were good he'd always want to know more. I had to dig deep, find the resolve to end this stalemate.

I swung my legs out of the bag. "I'm just not feeling well this morning. Inhaled too much smoke, stayed up too late, I don't know. How's the coffee coming along?"

"Almost ready." Russell Pruitt turned his back, pouring hot water over the drip cone that fed into the mug.

I stared at the handle of the butcher knife protruding from the backpack.

Stab him, Constance told me. *Upward stroke between the ribs on the right. Hit his kidney and he'll never get up again.*

That wasn't my style, and I was the one in charge. But maybe there was something I could do to even the odds.

I padded swiftly over to his hoodie sweatshirt hanging off the corner of the bunk and rifled through the pockets, one eye on Russell Pruitt's back. My hand closed around the cylinder of nitro pills and I slid it into my pocket. I was bending over my boots by the front door when he turned back. "I'll take the rope today," I said. "Barefoot wasn't very comfortable."

"Good," Russell Pruitt said, bringing me a mug of black

coffee. "I wasn't going to offer that to you again. We went too slow. I heard there's an old *heiau* on the ridge back a ways; I think we should go find it. Your reservations call for you to leave tomorrow, right?"

"Right." I took a sip of the coffee—delicious—and considered what Bruce was likely doing. He'd probably blown my phone call off as some sort of DTs panic attack. But in the morning, he'd want to check on me. He'd try my cell, and it would go immediately to voice mail. Then he'd call Aloha House and find out I'd never been there. That's when he'd crank up a rescue operation, probably by sending the Park Service to the cabin to see what was going on.

So all I had to do was get through today, and Russell Pruitt had promised not to kill me today. Hopefully the Park Service would come soon, and it wouldn't turn into a situation with Russell Pruitt holding me hostage in the cabin. I laced the boots up around the elastic bottoms of my now-filthy sweatpants. I still had the flashlight and the barbeque lighter down in there, but wondered if that had been a wasted effort.

Russell Pruitt brought the steaming bowls of cinnamon-laced, prune-filled oatmeal over to the table.

"Wow, so healthy. My mom would approve." I stirred the delicious-looking porridge.

"You never talk about your parents," Russell Pruitt said. "Tell me about them." He blew on his oatmeal, his lips a small pink Cupid's bow in the mass of his face.

"Ha. Tricky, you." I waggled my spoon at him. "Still trying to psych me into telling my story."

"No, really. I'm interested."

Now that I'd thought through the situation and knew I had his promise I'd have today and had a reasonable hope the Park Service would find me before it was over, I became a little expansive. "My parents weren't very interesting. It was having beautiful twin girls that made them interesting."

"So what happened to them after Constance died?"

I was hungry, and I knew I needed my strength, but the question killed my appetite. "Your questioning technique needs work. Try nonthreatening and open-ended when your client first starts to talk."

Russell Pruitt ducked his head, sheepish. "Sorry. Tell me more."

"My mother was a homemaker and working mom of that era—you know, the late seventies." I took a bite of the oatmeal. Somehow he'd remembered to bring brown sugar, and the flavors were exquisite. I let them roll around my mouth. "Mmm. Anyway, she was a legal secretary, worked during the day while we were at school. Wore those silky blouses with the built-in bows at the neck." I gestured. Russell Pruitt shook his head, brow wrinkled. "Before your time. My dad was a midlevel bank exec. We had a very nice, middle-class American upbringing. Girl Scouts, piano lessons. We weren't poor, but we weren't rich either."

"So what happened after Constance died?"

I took another bite, chewed. Set my spoon down. Picked up my mug of black coffee, sipped. "It all fell apart."

"How so?"

"Constance was everything to us." I looked down at the surface of the oatmeal, stirred it. I'd always liked the creamy colors of oatmeal. I decided in that moment that if I lived to get my new place, that would be the color of the walls. Maybe I'd do a little sponge painting for the texture. "Mom and Dad were no longer the parents of identical twin girls. They were parents who'd tragically lost the daughter with all the sparkle. They fought. They blamed themselves, then each other. They divorced. Pretty common scenario when a child dies."

"Go on. Is that what got you into psychology?" He'd finished already and turned around on the bench.

"I think I was always trying to understand. Find my way as the twin who was left behind." I stopped talking and ate rapidly, filling my stomach so it would settle. The oatmeal landed and coated it like cement in a mixer. I got up and ran water over the dish. "I want to put another log in the stove before we go, so it's warm when we get back."

Russell Pruitt, leaning over and putting on his enormous hiking boots, nodded. I went into the closet stacked high with Pres-to-Logs and dropped the nitro pills down behind the stack. It wouldn't do for him to decide to check where they were and then find them on me. Coming back out with a log, I found Russell Pruitt watching me.

I ignored him, brushing by with no hint of my thundering heart. Getting those pills back out, even if you knew where they were, would take some doing. I wondered why I'd even gone through with this potentially hazardous decision—and knew it was Constance pushing me, like she always had, to take some action. I was the one who liked to let things unfold.

At least I hadn't tried to stab Russell Pruitt in the kidney. That would not have ended well. *You might still need to use the knife,* Constance said. *You might not think he's a psychopath, but I do.*

"I'm the psychologist, not you," I muttered.

"What did you say?" Pruitt handed me a plastic water bottle.

"Nothing. Just talking to myself."

"Did you bring a camera? I'm planning to take some photos."

"You know perfectly well I didn't. I had only the one in my phone, and you know what happened to that."

"It's your own fault," Pruitt said, as every abuser says to their victim. "Put your wrist out."

He tied the rope around my wrist and then tied it to his belt loop. It felt strangely intimate to be so connected, and I fortified myself with Constance's rage at being restrained—

Stockholmed or not, I was this man's prisoner and I better not forget it.

We walked outside for the first time that day. The nene had come back, and they chortled up, ducking their heads, picking their way across the grass with their mincing gait. Much smaller than Canada geese, their coloring still marked them as distant cousins. Their voices were sweet, gentle. I squatted down, and they circled me while Russell Pruitt locked the cabin.

"The trail is this way." Pruitt pointed up the grassy slope behind the cabin.

We set out. The path led through a series of empty camp-sites. I paid attention to it because I had to—rocky and poorly formed, it was clearly not the thoroughfare we'd fol-lowed through the center of the crater.

It felt great to hike without the burden of the backpack. I looked out over the swath of lava being tamed by hardy native plants. We were circling back toward the heart of the crater.

No photo of Haleakala seemed to convey—and looking from the rim just couldn't show—the utter scope and vastness of the crater. Every hundred yards or so was some completely new, spectacular combination of vivid colors, arc of sky, land reduced to its purest forms in every shade from umber to gold. I stumbled, looking, and the rope yanked tight and abraded my wrist.

"Shit!" I exclaimed.

"I'm sorry." Pruitt untied the rope as I held my sore wrist with the other hand. "I don't think this is necessary."

"Thank you." I rubbed the abrasion circling my wrist. "It isn't."

My eyes tracked around the rugged lava—at ten thousand feet, out of shape, and with no hikers anywhere near us—I wasn't going anywhere but following in his wake like a little tender boat. Russell Pruitt got out his camera, took some vista shots. It was a nice little point-and-shoot Olympus.

"Smile." He pointed it at me.

I smiled, rubbing my rope-burned wrist. *Keep the giant happy; look for your chance*, Constance reminded me.

"Where's the *heiau*?" I asked as we kept walking, beginning to loop to the left, back toward the main trail.

I took a slug of water and felt the familiar pinch of the

boots as I put my fists into the back of my hips, arching upward. It was great not to be carrying the backpack and not to have the rope on my wrist anymore.

But I worried that we were getting so far from the cabin and that the Park Service would come while we were gone. That didn't seem like a good idea—maybe they'd just leave after seeing my backpack with the permit on it. How would they know anything was amiss with my roommate? I felt anxiety beginning as a nervous whisper under my sternum.

"Where are we going? And how long is it going to take?"

"You're worse than a kid on a road trip," Pruitt said. "I don't really know. Haven't seen any signs of the *heiau*. But it seems like we're looping back toward the main trail, so we might as well keep going forward."

I looked at his looming back resentfully. This was not going to be an idle morning amble; it was turning into a real hike. Oh well. No way out but through.

We circled through a gray sand field and undulated down a long incline, circling around a cinder cone to find one of the Park Service's brown-and-white signs: HOLUA CABIN: TWO MILES marked a merge with the main trail.

I remembered passing through this junction, an area of particularly spectacular formations. I took another pull off my water bottle, looking around for any other hikers—no such luck. The crater was as empty and enormous as ever.

"I'll be ready for lunch at this rate," I said as we approached the huge hole fenced in by a low guardrail we'd passed the day before, where the ceiling of an underground lava tube had broken in, leaving a deep shaft. A sign nearby proclaimed DANGER.

We'd walked by without hardly looking at it last time, but this time Russell Pruitt got out his little camera, took a picture of the scene: two humped cinder cones that reminded me of a Bactrian camel, the pit between them, the bare sand trail winding back toward Holua Cabin.

Russell Pruitt stepped close to the barrier, leaning down to shoot inside the hole. His flash lit that depthless-looking blackness and I came up beside him.

"Can you see the bottom?" I peered down.

"No. It's really deep." He slid the camera into his pocket, and suddenly his enormous ham hand was on my shoulder. "It looks dangerous." His voice trembled. His hand felt hot, very unpleasant. I shrugged it off.

"Yeah, looks like the Park Service thinks so too." I pointed to the sign that said DANGER.

"I bet they wouldn't find you here."

"What?" I turned, blinking. His face had gone that tell-tale gray that spoke of stress and a lack of oxygen, but that wasn't what had me scrambling backward, stumbling in the sand. "What did you say?"

"I thought of this last night." Sweat had sprung out on Russell Pruitt's face, pearly, greasy beads of sweat that shone in the bright sunlight overhead. Details were very clear in my hyper-focused vision.

I hadn't infected him with hope after all.

He reached for me and I leaped back, turning to flee, my boots heavy and clumsy, kicking up sand and refusing to obey fast enough. He got a handful of my shirt and it yanked tight against my throat, but now I was getting some traction in the sand, fight-or-flight had fully kicked in, and I swiveled, leaning over so he tore the T-shirt right off over my head.

I spun and kept going, feeling a warm breeze on my bare

skin. I felt a surge of strength so great I saw my liberty nearby and true, my body twenty years old again, competing for the race of my life.

The grasp on my hair that stopped my flight was so abrupt I thought my neck had snapped as he yanked me back.

He was going to kill me, and my main feeling was shocked betrayal. "You promised me another day!" I yelled.

There was no reason to hold anything back anymore, so I fought like hell.

I kicked him in the knee, went for his groin, reached for his eyes with the sharp hooks of my thumbs, uttering a feral growl I didn't even know was my own voice. The trouble was, he was so very tall, so long armed, that as he held me by that fistful of hair, I was too far away to get in any meaningful damage—much like dangling an angry kitten by the scruff of its neck.

Still, I scratched and clawed at his wrists, trying to loosen his grip. He then grabbed one of my wrists as well as my hair and jerked me off my feet. I hit the ground and took a faceful of sand. He flipped me over and turned, towing me back toward the hole.

I opened my mouth and screamed, as loud as I could. Repeatedly.

It was such an awful bellowing wail, I realized I'd never given voice to a full scream in my entire life.

"Help me!" I screamed, remembering words were more useful in getting assistance.

He let go of my wrist and smacked me. It was like being hit with a frying pan—my whole face wobbled and swelled instantly with the force of it, and I shut up, stunned. He got hold of my other hand and hauled me toward the oubliette in the middle of the crater. This was really it, the moment I looked death in the eye.

"You promised, Russell Pruitt!" I cried, tasting iron from a split lip. "You promised me one more day!"

"I lied," he said, panting with the effort of dragging me through the sand. "You know I'm good at lying."

I dug my boots in and tried to slow him. I thrashed from side to side, trying to break his hold. A scene from a martial arts movie came back to me, where the heroine dug in her feet and stood up so forcefully she broke the attacker's hold—but this wasn't Hollywood, and I was a nearing fifty-year-old alcoholic who weighed in at one-third of her attacker. Words had always stood me in better stead. I kept writhing and digging, slowing down the inevitable as I said, "Bruce Ohale is my police chief on the Big Island. He'll be looking for me, and you won't get away with this. Please, we can do something else."

"I know who he is, and I know you spoke to him. That's why I had to move up my timetable," Russell Pruitt said.

We'd reached the barrier, and he leaned against it, obviously winded by our struggle. "I figure my chances are fifty-fifty on getting away with it. I'll clean up, leave your stuff in the cabin with a suicide note, and go out Sliding Sands instead of Switchbacks. Anyway, I was always willing to chance getting caught—what do I have to lose, right? I'm already dying. Remember those temp clerks they thought my dad killed?"

I couldn't nod, couldn't move. The grip on my hair was paralyzingly painful, my wrist smashed in his massive hand, and I was facedown on the sand, the toes of my boots dug in. What was this, a confession of some sort?

Keep him talking! Constance yelled in my inner ear. *Buy time!*

"What are you telling me?" I turned my face, spat sand off my lips.

"I actually didn't need therapy to figure out who I was, Dr. Wilson. Dad and I—we killed those women together. But thanks for the voyage of self-discovery. I know you tried to help me."

He reached down and hoisted me up under the armpits. I flailed and writhed in vain.

"You're acting like a psychopath, and that's the same as being one. How sad." My voice trembled with all the grief I'd ever shared, ever carried—for myself, for my clients, for this moment of my own death when I still had so much to live for.

"I didn't want to be. He made me one," Russell Pruitt said, and lifted me. "I can't help myself. I'm sorry."

"That's bullshit! Even psychopaths have choice!" I kicked backward with everything I had and got him good in the shin. I heard him grunt. *"I don't want to die! Not now, not like this!"*

Constance and I were united in our cry. I'd given all I had to the fight—but none of it was enough to stop his savage heave. He was just so much stronger.

I flew like a rag doll over the barrier.

Chapter 20

*I*flopped over the low wooden fence, my left arm trailing, and I grabbed hold of the lowest rail as my body hit the packed-gravel edge of the pit with a bone-jarring crunch. Sand embedded with sharp stones bit into my bare chest and face and my legs swung around like a pendulum, gravity hauling me into that dark maw.

I added my right hand to hold desperately on to the splintery, rickety wood of the lower railing, a degree of my weight still supported by the lip of the cavern curving out from under my bare torso. I scrabbled with my boots on the side of the lava tube and heard the *thunk* and *tinkle* of a thousand pebbles and rocks bouncing away into infinity.

And, miracle of miracles, my right boot caught on some-thing—an embedded rock. It held, supported my weight. I slowed my movements, set my left boot tentatively on the protrusion as well, and leaned forward flat against the side of the pit.

I lifted my cheek off the stones and sand of the edge and looked up to see what the giant was doing.

He wasn't there. The edge arched up from under my arm-pits, blocking my view of anything above the guardrail—but I was surprised his face wasn't looming over me, waiting to peel my fingers off the railing one at a time. Nothing but that mocking baby-blue sky, dotted with poufy white clouds, looked down at me.

Pruitt's disappearance could only be good. Maybe he'd been squeamish in the end and hadn't wanted to see me disappear into blackness, hear my screams cut off. I shud-dered with the power of the image of my broken body lying hundreds of feet down at the bottom of the lava tube in the pitch dark. More likely, Pruitt had just hurried off to set up his escape.

I leaned as far forward as I could, pressing myself into the side, and by doing so I could let go of the railing with my strained left hand, my legs supporting me. I shook the hand, feeling cramps forming along my fingers and forearms, the nerves jangling with tiny electric shocks. I put the hand back up after I'd hung it down for a moment and had circulation again—and then I did the same with my right hand.

I was delicately balanced on my protrusion, and I could stand there, with support of one hand or the other, for a while.

I began to wonder how long a while was going to be.

I could feel panic beating at the back of my mind with fluttery soft wings—and Constance was the one who pushed the tide of betraying moths back into their closet.

You've been given another chance. Stay alive one minute at a time. Call out every few minutes. Everyone hiking down this trail comes over to look down the hole; someone will come.

"Help me!" I called. The hole and the sand seemed to swallow my voice, and my throat was chalky. I worked up some spit and called again. "Help! I'm in the hole!"

Okay then, this was the routine. Call twice. Give the arms

each a break. Give the legs a shake.

Shaking my left leg, I felt the cylinder of the barbeque lighter against my calf. Could the flashlight or the barbeque lighter help me climb out of the pit?

The little penlight seemed useless.

I hunched up onto the side, resting my cheek on sun-warmed sand and stones, leaned as much of my body weight on the soil as I could, consciously slowing down my respiration.

In through the nose, out through the mouth. All was Zen. I was in control of my body and my emotions.

When it seemed like five minutes had gone by, I rose, collected enough spit in my mouth to work my vocal cords, and yelled, "Help me! In the pit, help me!"

Then, like a prairie dog, I held myself up, listening. All I could see was blue sky above me, the slope of the hole, and the painted wood of the barrier. I heard nothing, not even the wind. The crater was funny that way—sound carried, but there was so little of it. I could only hope my voice was escaping the black hole of absorption that was the sand-lined lava tube.

I went through my routine. Flatten against the side. Shake out left arm for several minutes. Switch arms. Shake right leg. Shake left leg.

Once again the barbeque lighter rattled inside my sweats and I wondered if I could use it. Narrower than the flashlight, perhaps I could work it into the soil, use it as a handhold to boost myself high enough to pull myself out of the pit. With my arms extended and limited upper-arm strength, doing so as I currently stood was out of the question.

I did my Zen rest for a full five minutes against the side, then went through the routine again. Call out. Shake out and recirculate each limb. Rest.

The sun was directly overhead, burning my scalp and exposed skin, and as the adrenaline ebbed out of my system, I became more and more aware of physical misery.

My swollen face ached, one of my teeth loosened from Russell Pruitt's openhanded slap. I could only imagine what would have happened if he'd actually punched me. My arms, exhausted and quivering, almost wrenched from their sockets, promised now and future reprisals. Bruises complained down my legs from the tumble over the side. I smelled of the urine I didn't even know I'd let go in that last moment of utter terror.

Standing in that stretched-out position began to send spasms of muscle pain up and down my back. The skin of my torso was scraped as if with a cheese grater and felt on fire. Thirst was beginning, like the tuning up of an orchestra that would build to a crescendo of suffering.

Actually, you got off light, Constance said. *You got in some good kicks and scratches on him. Got trace under your nails. He could have strangled you, smothered you, beaten you to death with a few blows, then thrown you in.*

She was right. I needed to stay positive, count my blessings. I almost burst into a fit of hysterical giggles but used my yoga breathing to control that.

The gradual weakening of my arms convinced me I had to try something with the barbeque lighter. I was having to shake and dangle them more and more often, and it occurred to me that it might be better to die trying something possibly stupid than die by simply being unable to hang on any longer.

I did my routine one more time before I was ready.

I began by inching more to the middle of the protrusion, so I could lift my left leg with more stability. I shook the lighter around until I was reasonably certain it was caught in the stretchy elastic of the sweatpants, then lifted my leg, curling it up as high toward my buttocks as I could and reaching down with my left arm.

All those long-ago yoga classes paid off a couple of tries later when I caught hold of my left ankle with my left hand. Groping along, I identified the shape of the lighter and eased it out of the elastic.

Holding the little bulb in my hand, I looked at the long steel wand with a sense of wonder. Could this fragile-looking piece of plastic and metal really be a piton I put my weight on? I flashed on that moment in the cabin when I'd wondered how the hell a barbeque lighter could do anything to help me.

I worked it into the soil about six inches above my right shoulder, then rested, recentering my feet, doing my breath-ing, imagining the molecules of my body opening to bond with the molecules of the ground, holding me effortlessly in place. I did my arms, did my legs, did my cries for help, then worked the pointy end of the lighter in another inch.

The soil, if you could call it that, was actually tightly packed layers of cinder, volcanic sand, and ash, all complicated by little glassy pebbles spewed like breath from the volcano in its heyday. Not easy to penetrate, but that was good in its way because I was going to be putting my body weight on it, and the last thing I needed was to knock it out and go sliding into the abyss.

Sliding into the abyss was actually beginning to seem appealing, and I knew that wasn't good. I calculated it had been about an hour since Russell Pruitt threw me in, and every fiber of my body was strained by this ordeal.

Fantasies of falling to a blissful death fluttered in the same dark place the panic had lurked, but Constance beat those back for me as I did my routine two more times until the eight inches of steel wand were buried in the rugged ground and only the plastic bulb with its metal banding protruded.

I wriggled it. The barbeque lighter was in solid. I could twist it in a circle, but leaning on it yielded only a few grains of falling sand.

I did an extra-long rest, followed by an extra-loud and -long calling for help, followed by one more shake out as I thought through what I'd do.

I would put my elbow up on the bulb.

I would push down on the lighter, using all my core strength, while pulling myself up with my left hand. I'd raise myself high enough to dig my knees into the side.

I'd push up with my knees and heave myself high enough to get my right arm hooked over the lowest bar.

Then I'd use my left hand to grasp the support pole and I'd heave myself through the lower bars onto the ground outside.

I took some deep breaths, filling my lungs, picturing the steps I'd take, feeling my heart accelerate to get ready—and I called out one more time. "Help me! In the pit! Help!"

Nothing happened. No one came. This trip had been remarkable in that way. It was up to me and Constance to get out of this situation. I did a couple more deep breaths, went through my shaking-out routine, and by now my heart was up to trip-hammer speed.

Panic fueled the jolt of adrenaline that fired all my circuits. I threw my elbow up on the striker, contracted my abs, hauled up my knees even as I pushed down with my right elbow and pulled up on the rail with my left hand.

My knees wouldn't get a purchase. A hail of pebbles and sand loosened as I heaved. I managed to wriggle and pull myself up anyway, by straining, trembling, frantic inches. The moment I had both elbows hooked over the lowest bar was one of the most triumphant of my life. From there I was able to get one knee up and eventually hoist myself grace-lessly through the railing to land face-first, flat on the sand.

Nothing had felt so good in my life. I spread my arms and legs, swung those poor abused limbs up and down in a sand angel shape and fell asleep like that for several minutes.

Thirst woke me up. I raised my head off the hot sand, looking around in vain for help. *What's up with this damned trail? People are supposed to come through here all day!* Constance bitched.

I pulled myself up to my knees, and that's when I saw Russell Pruitt.

Chapter 21

I stayed where I was, one hand on the barrier surrounding the pit, using it for support. Pruitt was lying face-up, and his eyes were closed. I looked around him and saw nothing but claw marks in the sand, his pockets turned out, some marks where his legs had spasmed, and a wet mark at his crotch.

I wasn't the only one to urinate when faced with dying. I felt better for that, somehow.

Throwing me into the pit had killed him. Served him right, I thought, even as guilt twisted my guts. He'd died without his medication, and that was my doing.

I crawled very slowly over to him, in case he was just

sunbathing by some freaky chance. It was hard to approach him at all, but I wanted to make sure.

"Russell Pruitt?" No response. His eyes didn't open behind his Coke-bottle glasses. I leaned over and pressed two fingers to his neck. The flesh was warm, imitating life, but it had a spongy quality as I pushed in. I felt a tiny dim flutter, and I lay my ear on his chest. I could hear his great, swollen, damaged heart struggling. A thready thump, a swish. Another. Another. His chest rose and fell with tiny reflexive breaths.

The sun glared down on us, the sand was hot, and there was no possible anything that could be done to save Russell Pruitt—but I somehow knew he'd been waiting for me.

I stretched out beside him, put my arm over that massive chest.

"I forgive you," I whispered in his ear. "You can go now. Good-bye, Russell Pruitt. Thanks for the journey of self-discovery."

I stroked his dark hair off his brow and lay my cheek on his massive chest. He sighed his last breath, a long, slow exhalation that didn't seem to end. His heart gave one last thump and swish. I lay beside him for a long time with my cheek on his chest.

When I sat up, there was a wet spot on his shirt. I'd cried for him.

I didn't know how I had any water left in my dehydrated body. I pressed my fingers into his neck one last time— nothing. The dents of my two fingers remained on his throat for a long moment.

Poor kid. He'd always been that, in spite of everything else he was.

I looked around for the water bottle I'd carried while we were hiking. There was a chance it had fallen out of my pocket and was still in the sand. Yes, I could see it, lying half-full in the dune marked by the gouges and scores of my battle with the giant.

Standing up, every muscle in my body aching, I staggered over to the bottle of water and took several large gulps. I left at least two good swallows for the way back to the cabin— because that's where I was going, that's where the Park Service would look for me, and that's where there was a good supply of boiled water. I picked up my crumpled T-shirt and put it back on.

I got on the trail and put one boot in front of the other on the way to Holua Cabin. I had nothing left physically but aches and pains and yet nothing in the world to do but get back to that cabin—so I walked.

A half hour later, three horses approached me at a trot. Bringing up the rear, big as a refrigerator and twice as reassuring, was Bruce Ohale.

I let my knees fold and crumpled onto the edge of the trail to rest. Bruce kicked his horse into gear and pulled up next to me.

"Dammit, Caprice!" he exclaimed, sliding off his mount. "You look like hell!" He fisted his hands on his hips—I could tell he was restraining himself from scooping me up.

"Been there, done that," I said. "You've got some *paniolo* in your blood, Bruce. I can tell." I guzzled my last sips of water, knowing there would be more. I pointed back the way I'd come for the benefit of the rangers on horses looking down at me. "There's a body up ahead by the lava tube pit. Russell Pruitt, aged twenty-two, dead of a preexisting heart condition."

The two rangers spurred their horses and covered us with dust as they moved off to investigate. Bruce squatted beside me. His face was clenched into a fist of worry. "Are you okay?"

"Never been better. I'm alive, I'm sober, and I'm stronger than I ever knew." I burst into dry sobbing—there were no tears left.

Bruce gave me a hug. It felt as wonderful as before.

I got to ride and Bruce walked the horse back to the cabin. The rangers called in Maui Police Department and the coroner, and they flew Russell Pruitt's body out on a helicopter. I watched it fly like a great mechanical dragonfly out of the crater with the yellow body basket fastened underneath. Russell Pruitt was so large his boots were hanging out of the basket—but that wouldn't have mattered to him anymore.

The rangers administered first aid, and finally, boots off, clothes changed, propped up in my bunk with an IV rehydrating me, I told Bruce my story.

At least, all that I was willing to tell.

"How did you find me?" Seeing Bruce ride toward me

Toby Neal

still felt like a mirage. I peeked at him sitting next to my bunk on the bench he'd dragged over, just to make sure he was real.

"I tried to ring you back several times after that weird call. No answer, like the phone was turned off. Called Aloha House. You hadn't checked in. Remembered you said you wanted to see Haleakala; called the ranger station. They said you'd hiked in alone, but I had a bad feeling, figured your stalker could have pinged your phone. I took the next flight out and got the rangers moving."

He'd done just as I'd imagined in my more hopeful moments.

"So, as you guessed, Russell Pruitt was the stalker." I took a sip of water. Even with the IV going, I was still thirsty.

"I thought as much." Bruce gestured to a tiny handheld recorder. "Okay if I tape this?"

"Sure." I filled him in on Russell Pruitt's background, how he'd targeted me. His gigantism, his revenge fixation, his quest for identity.

"He pretended he was going to let me live." I took another sip of water. My lips were dry, and I found my voice thickening. "He lied. He was a very good liar."

"You said he was obsessed with psychopaths because of his father's diagnosis. Do you think he was a psychopath?" Bruce leaned forward on the chair, his hands loosely clasped between his knees. I could see the tribal tattoos on the insides of his arms, and once again I wondered where they went.

"He thought he was. I actually don't. And that's the saddest of a lot of really sad things." I sat up, leaning my back against the wall and crossing my legs on the bunk. "He was damaged. Traumatized by an environment of domestic abuse, his mother's murder, his father making him participate in murder, a life in foster homes, and the final straw, his gigantism. He used his obsession with 'dealing justice' to me as a coping device to handle the terrible circumstances of his life. He was dying, and he was having a crisis of meaning. Trying to find out who he was. Trying to see if he was his father."

I covered my face with my hands. I was unable to think of Russell Pruitt with anything but a terrible, complicated grief.

He tried his best to kill you, Constance said. *You don't owe him shit.*

"So he had an enlarged, weak heart," Bruce said. This was what I'd told the rangers, what I'd told Bruce earlier.

"Yes. The exertion of throwing me into the hole did him in." I remembered that last long sigh of his breath. "In the end, I killed him."

"Caprice." Bruce took my chilled hands in his big warm ones. "It's not your fault."

"No. It is. He had heart medication. I took it and hid it." I pulled a hand out of his and pointed a trembling finger at the closet with the Pres-to-Logs. "It's hidden back behind the logs in there."

A long moment passed. Bruce held my gaze with hard brown cop eyes. "That doesn't change a thing. As far as he was concerned, he killed you. It was only after he threw you in the pit that natural consequences took over and he got what he had coming. You'd have been justified in taking a lot stronger self-defense measures than hiding his medication."

I had no response to this, but there was some relief in hearing those words so strongly spoken. Bruce got up and went into the closet. I heard him moving the logs. "Lower right corner," I called.

Right or wrong, I knew I'd killed Russell Pruitt—and I'd have to live with that for the rest of my life.

Bruce reappeared, carrying the bottle of nitro, and walked over to push the Off button on the recorder. "There will be a hearing with the coroner after Russell's autopsy," he said. "I'm tempted to just throw this medication away myself and spare you the hassle, but neither of our consciences would let that stand. Don't worry. If you'd shot the bastard right in the face it would have been okay."

I looked down. "I'm sorry I didn't go to Aloha House to get sober."

Bruce gave a bark of laughter. "Whatever works, and I'm guessing this adventure worked. Are you sober?"

"Stone cold. And planning to stay that way."

"Then no worries." He sat beside me on the bunk, an awkward endeavor with his size. He slung an arm over my shoulders. "Let's get you home and back to work. You've got people who need you."

My eyes prickled with tears—his words warmed me right down to my bruised bones. Being needed was my personal kryptonite, always had been. "I'm going to be making some big changes when I get home. I'm going to need a few weeks."

"I expected nothing less. We'll be waiting."

"Thanks, Bruce. For everything."

Our words felt layered with meaning.

Because they are layered with meaning, Constance said. *You like him.*

I had to admit that, as usual, she was right.

Chapter 22

*T*wo weeks later, I handed Detective Freitas her folder—missing the notes I'd written on. "So sorry I missed the window for doing these profiles on your case. I promise it won't happen again."

"It's understandable, after all you've been through. We got the case covered." How I'd come to be hiking Haleakala Crater in the middle of a job was skimmed over. "How're you doing? You look wonderful."

Freitas's big brown eyes were still concerned, as we sat in my counseling office and she took in the changes I'd made. I knew I was still thin, but the bruising on my face was gone and I'd had my hair cut and colored. It was a tousled mix of blond, everything from caramel to cream, and the new look did good things for my skin and eyes. Dressed in a sky-blue silk wrap dress and kitten heels, I was debuting Dr. Wilson's new professional image.

The polo shirts and twill skirts had joined a lot of other stuff at the Goodwill. Constance's influence was all over my life, and I felt more myself than ever. I was listening to that little internal voice saying "yes" to this, and "no" to that.

"Making some major changes, but they're good ones," I said, folding my hands over my knee. "How's the department?"

"Something's always cookin' in paradise," Freitas said with her big smile. "We've got some good cases. It's a living."

"There's a lot more to life than catching criminals. I hope you're taking time for some of those things."

"Sounds like time-tested wisdom. What are you doing in that area?"

I smiled. "Wouldn't you like to know."

Freitas laughed, standing and swinging the pebbled-leather briefcase containing the folder over her shoulder.

"It's great to see you looking so good. We'll be calling you again."

"You do that. Bye, Kamani." I followed her to the door. She hugged me, that powerful squeeze from strong, toned arms—and this time it just felt good, a reminder I was loved more than I knew.

I shut the door behind her.

This had been my first day back in the office, and it had gone well. I'd made some changes here too, bringing in some of my favorite art pieces from Hidden Palms and my sheepskin bedroom rug, which lay invitingly in front of the sofa for clients to sink their toes into.

Detective Freitas was my last meeting of the day, which had been productive as I reconnected with each of my regular clients. I'd decided to throw away the items Russell Pruitt had gifted me with, except for the WORLD'S GREAT-EST GRANDMA mug, which I'd returned to Mrs. Kunia. In the excitement of telling me about her husband's rescue by the rangers at his hunting cabin, she'd put it in her purse without comment. They were turning a corner in their grief at last, and she'd brought her granddaughter, Maile, in today.

My phone beeped with a message, and I listened to a voice mail from my real estate agent detailing upcoming showings for Hidden Palms, which was already attracting some solid offers. I closed the office windows, locked the door, and activated the alarm, clicking down the wooden steps in my pretty heels. I walked past the red gingers, which I'd had cut to waist height for visibility.

I unlocked the Mini Cooper and got in. Sighed with happiness, breathing in natural vanilla air freshener and leather cleaner. Coming back from Haleakala Crater, I'd walked through Hidden Palms and chosen only the things I really needed and left the rest without looking back.

The car I really needed, and I'd sent it to be detailed. That was the new way I was living—only the essentials. And those, lovingly cared for.

I turned the key, and the engine started with its low purring, a sound that somehow reminded me of the nene in the crater—a happy little conversation, just beginning. I pulled out and got back into the Hilo traffic, thinking over my various cases with the sound of Ottmar Liebert's guitar rarefying the air.

I pulled up in front of my apartment building on Banyan Drive immediately on Hilo Bay, sandwiched between a couple of hotels. A little trade wind off the Bay lifted my hair and tossed it around as I beeped the Mini locked and walked up the path. Bordered by trimmed *naupaka* shrubs, it was a small building but well maintained. I wound around the cement walk to the entrance of my ground-floor apartment and unlocked the door.

Hector sat on the tile in the entry, his tail arcing back and forth. He greeted me with loud accusations.

"You can go out. Just in the front yard," I reminded him, slipping my little heels off and setting them on the rack. I walked across the gleaming bamboo floors to the front deck, opened the slider, and let Hector out—he'd ignored his cat door in the screen window. Still piqued, he refused to acknowledge me and walked by, tail twitching. I had the lawn out front staked with one of those sonic pet barriers, and I followed him out onto my sweet little deck. The Adirondack chairs from the Palms house sat at inviting angles for me to look at the smooth evening waters of Hilo Bay.

Hector walked over the immaculate grass to the sonic

barrier and yowled. The coqui frogs in a nearby banyan were just tuning up, and he and the ubiquitous tree frogs seemed to have a meaningful exchange.

"Russell Pruitt told me you'd get used to this," I told Hector, feeling a pang as I spoke the giant's name. "We're both making some adjustments. It's a good thing."

He disagreed vociferously.

I walked back into the apartment and into the kitchen, a little galley style with a breakfast bar open to the rest of the condo. I poured myself a Perrier, dropped a couple of ice cubes and a slice of lime into it.

I hadn't taken much from the Palms house. The good leather couch and that comfy chair for reading. A particularly fine painting Chris had done in high school hung over the couch, a seascape of Punalu`u Beach, with a turtle sunning itself on the black sand in the foreground. One bedroom I'd made into a guest room/office in hopes Chris would join me at the holidays. The other was mine, equipped with a new queen bed—just right for a woman alone.

I walked back outside. Hector was walking the perimeter of the fence, complaining, but when he saw me sit in the Adirondack chair, he came back, climbed into my lap, and turned on his motorboat purr. Hilo Bay was settling into evening glass, candy-pink clouds reflected in the water gilded by sunset happening on the Kona side of the island. Palm fronds clattered, the coqui croaked a jungle chorus, and mynahs chattered in their sleep tree nearby. This was where I'd always wanted to be—on the ocean, wide open and fresh. Sipping my Perrier, I even spotted the plume of a humpback's breath near the mouth of the Bay.

I loved being here, in this cozy little space. I didn't miss anything but a few memories from the Palms house.

I got my phone out and speed-dialed my mentor, Dr. Judy Dennis. She'd been one of my instructors at university and a professional, then personal, mentor after she retired. She was also in AA and my new sponsor.

"Hi, Cappy." She was the only one to call me that, and it made me happy to hear her husky smoker's voice say my name.

"Hi, Judy. Well, I made it through my first day back at work."

"Excellent. Whatcha drinking?"

"Perrier with lime." I stroked Hector, and he blinked his crystal-blue eyes at me. They still reminded me of Richard's eyes, but I hoped they wouldn't someday—those were Chris's eyes too.

"Good girl. The first day back at work is hard and the evening routine even harder."

"It helps so much to be in the new place. I knew I had to get out of the Palms house the minute I got out of the crater if I was going to stay sober. This is so much better." Even as I spoke, one of my neighbors, retired Mr. Gonsalez, wandered across the lawn with his binoculars—he kept a close eye on the humpback activity in the Bay. He raised a hand in greeting, which I returned.

"I'm not alone out in the boondocks. I'm right in town. I see people. I'm a part of the community." I stroked Hector's soft fur, drawing my fingers along his seal-point ears. He shut his eyes and turned up the purr volume. "I'm away from a lot of my triggers."

"How bad were your cravings today?"

"About a three and a half." We used a five-point Likert scale for me to report daily craving levels, with one the worst ever and five completely craving free. I also kept a log of my triggers and how I handled them. "I want to talk about Russell Pruitt."

"It's about time." I heard Judy drag on her cigarette; she'd told me I could be her sponsor when she finally quit smoking. "What brought him up?"

"He's always there. Taken up residence in the mental closet Constance used to live in." I gave a bark of a laugh. "I couldn't get her back in there if I tried."

"I've always thought the way you disappeared her from your life wasn't healthy."

"It wasn't a choice early on. I missed her too much. The pain was too bad. I put her away because it was so hard to go on without her as only one of a pair of shoes. But in the crater, I realized she was always with me; she lives on in my very DNA. And she has very good taste."

"So you are bringing her out of Shadow. And now Russell Pruitt is in Shadow, much bigger and scarier."

"The key is to know and own your Shadow, make friends with it." A concept out of Jungian psychology I'd always liked. "Also, no one could be stronger and scarier than Constance." I remembered her voice telling me to stab Russell Pruitt. "I was afraid that if I let her out, really remembered and experienced her, my twin would take me over. I realized that wasn't the case. I could love and embrace all Constance was—because she's me too. Ultimately, she gave me the strength to deal with Russell Pruitt."

"You still feel guilty about his death." I'd told her the bare bones—that I hadn't actively killed him while he'd certainly tried to murder me—but I'd taken his life in a passive form of murder.

"I know I shouldn't feel guilty. No matter how I come at the situation we were in—legally, morally, mental-health-wise—I know I had to defend myself by any means I could find. The coroner cleared me. The ME said that nitro medicine or no nitro, his heart was in bad shape and he could have gone anytime."

"So why do you feel guilty?"

"I don't know. He was narcissistic, twisted, and he took me prisoner and did abusive things to me. And yet, until the moment when he was hauling me by my hair to the pit, I didn't really believe he'd hurt me. I had to keep trying to hold on to my defenses. I felt a real affection for him."

"You're the mother of a son close to his age. You felt a degree of responsibility for what happened to him. You're a kind and compassionate woman. It's natural."

"The psychologist I talked to said I was Stockholmed."

"I actually think that's too simplistic an explanation for what happened between you two."

I knew that was true.

I found myself petting Hector too hard, but he just kneaded my lap, potentially ruining my new silk dress. I didn't care. I felt closer to understanding what had happened between Russell Pruitt and me.

"We were on parallel journeys. He was trying to find out if he was his father, trying to resolve his past by confronting me. I was trying to find out who I was, too—make peace with my grief over my twin, with losing my husband and role as a mom. Trying to find out who I was without alcohol. By the end, even our bodies were in sync."

"That's amazing. What a great case study it would make." Her scholar's mind was always analyzing. "You both resolved things you came to resolve—and in that incredible setting."

"I know. But I have this guilt. I lived and he didn't. I lived and Constance didn't. I feel like it's supposed to mean something."

"You know about survivor guilt. You can ascribe meaning to this, or not. Be aware of your process." Judy was a sharp cookie. She didn't get to be head of the psychology department at a major university by accident. "I'm interested to see what you make of your life, with this release from the past, uncharted future without Richard, and kicking booze in the teeth."

I gave a shaky laugh. "Think I'll do some journaling about it. See what emerges. I was already doing good work I'm proud of, so that doesn't need improvement."

"You might be surprised," Judy said. "Call me tomorrow, same time. Full report, babe." She hung up.

I sighed, pressed the Off button. Switched to my photo and video cache. I'd purged pictures with Richard out of the phone. I thought someday I'd be able to appreciate all he'd been to me, what he'd brought into my life, but this wasn't that time. So now I just had pictures of Chris and my little cache of video documentary I was making for my future self.

I'd been able to save the SIM card—it had ridden through my travails in my pocket, and the data had transferred to my new phone. I thumbed to the video called "Haleakala Crater Cabin."

I pressed the little arrow key, and my haggard image looked me in the eye.

"Caprice, you're a wreck. You've been given another chance at life." I listened to the riveting monologue ending with, "I'm doing it. I'm suffering now so you, me in the future, can have a better life. Don't fuck it up."

I didn't plan to.

The doorbell rang, an unfamiliar buzz. I stood, and Hector complained, following me as I applied my eye to the peephole.

I felt my pulse pick up. I opened the door. "Hi, Bruce. What brings you here?"

He pushed his Oakleys atop his buzz-cut head. He was holding a fern plant, a glorious one lush with curling, intricate fronds. "Wanted to check the security on the new place."

I laughed, standing back. "Come on in. Not worried about that anymore."

He handed me the fern. "Congrats on the move."

"It's really a very good thing." I set the plant on the counter. "Thanks so much; this is gorgeous. I'd offer you a drink but—you know I don't have any. I can get you some Perrier."

"Wasn't checking up on that," he said. "But I'll take some, thanks." He'd walked to the front of the apartment. "Great view, great spot. Do you have a broom handle to put in the slider at night?"

"Seriously, Bruce, the crisis is over," I said, bending into the fridge to get the bottle of Perrier and the limes. When I stood back up he'd rejoined me in the kitchen, and I could swear he'd been looking at my rear, even though he cut his eyes away before I could be sure.

My cheeks went hot. I busied myself cutting the limes and making the drinks as he turned away, taking in the space. "Nice painting."

"My son did it. He's very talented, got a creative side." I

handed him the glass, and our fingers brushed, which activated a tingle somewhere I forgot tingles could be activated.
"Want to sit outside?"

"Sure." We went out to the deck again and sat in the Adirondack chairs. He put his head back against the solid wood
frame, and I let myself look at him over the top of my glass.

He looked tired. Being a station chief was no small responsibility, and I could see it in the tiny puckers of stress
beside his mouth, in a line between his brows that never
really left. He adjusted his big body in the chair and sighed.
"Feels good to smell the ocean."

"That's why I'm here. The whales have been jumping in
the Bay every evening."

"Would you go out with me?" he asked suddenly, as if
he had to just say it. He turned his head, still resting against
the back of the chair, and looked at me. "I'd like to—spend
more time with you."

Heat came wafting back over me like a hot flash—what
the hell. I was menopausal, so maybe that was what it was.
"I'd like that." I slurped my Perrier clumsily.

"Good." He sipped his Perrier. "I find myself thinking

about you a lot."

"Huh. Really." We talked on the phone almost daily since the crater, but I hadn't let myself really think about where things were going—it had started to matter too much.

"Yeah. I like you a lot. You're an amazing woman, Caprice Wilson. Way out of my league."

"Ha-ha," I said. My heart was thundering. "Wrong about that. Just a middle-aged alcoholic divorcée."

"Educated. Beautiful. Smart. Courageous as hell." He took a sip of the Perrier, shook his head, set the drink down on the side table. "Mostly I really like hugging you." He patted his lap. "Come on over here."

"I thought you'd never ask," I said, getting up out of my chair. Bruce folded me in against him. My cheek rested on his chest, and I heard the thump and swish of his heart. I closed my eyes and remembered the last faltering beat of that other great big heart.

Good-bye, Russell Pruitt. Rest in peace.

Bruce's heart beat on—strong and regular. I hoped I'd hear it for a very long time.

Acknowledgements:

Some authors don't do acknowledgements. Personally, I love them both as a reader and as a writer. It's my chance to talk directly to my readers and explain a little about the book, where and why and what the heck for. Readers have let me know they like this too.

I've known since Dr. Wilson first appeared in Blood Orchids that I wanted to do a book with her as the protagonist, something more personal than the Lei books, something that revealed a "glimpse under the robes" of a working psychologist and showed more of the spunky, conventional yet unconventional woman she is.

In Jungian dreamwork, all the figures in a dream are thought to represent aspects of self—and in my writing, my characters, particularly my main characters, have been a chance to "actualize" different aspects that never will be shown in real life (and thank God for that). I think every writer will acknowledge that writing gives voice to imagined worlds within and that's one of the reasons we write.

Dr. Wilson, however, is more personal and close to the "real me" than other characters, probably because she's in my profession and near my age. Sometimes, when she talks it's directly me speaking—for instance when she talked about joining clients in their pain. "That's it exactly," I said aloud, as Caprice Wilson put words to the unique calling of therapy and how it costs—and how it gives back. Her dry humor is also a bit how I roll in real life.

But, lest I start rumors: I am happily married for twenty-seven years to the amazing Mike Neal and I'm the oldest of four sisters in a wacky and wonderful family, the mother of two awesome well-adjusted twentysomethings (not twins!), and a social drinker who wishes she didn't have to count calories every minute.

I was also excited to be able to use a fuller range of concepts, ideas, and vocabulary. Much as I love Lei, she's more of an intuitive than intellectual character, and Dr. Wilson, with her degrees and expertise, was fun to write from without worrying about notes from my editor like I get on the Lei series: "Lei would not say "gloaming. She probably has never heard of it." Boo.

I greatly enjoyed this foray in a different direction, while being aware it's a risk and not all of you are going to love it. That said, I wanted to explore some deeper themes in this book. If any book clubs get inspired to read Unsound, here are some questions I was exploring through this story that you might consider discussing:

* What is the nature of psychopathy and is it inherited?

* Is anyone really "good" or "evil"?

* Was Russell Pruitt a psychopath or was Dr. Wilson wrong about him?

* Why did Dr. Wilson become attached to Russell?

* How are ideas both like free radicals or viruses?

* What is the nature of hope, and how it can it chain us to a certain longed-for outcome?

* Why is an extreme setting like Haleakala Crater a good place for a book like this?

* How do you feel about addictions and the people who have them?

* What do you think of the feeling Caprice had that she was the "copy" identical twin?

* How did the complication of Caprice's grief for her lost twin add to her character?

These companion books each have their own flavor and

feeling, one that the main character dictates. I definitely plan to do more with Dr. Wilson and her clients. I think they have a lot to teach us.

With much aloha,

Toby Neal, August 2013

Sign up for news of upcoming books at
http://www.tobyneal.net/

Watch for these titles:
Lei Crime Series:

Blood Orchids (Book 1)
Torch Ginger (Book 2)
Black Jasmine (Book 3)
Broken Ferns (Book 4)
Twisted Vine (Book 5)
Shattered Palms (Book 6)

Companion Series:

Stolen in Paradise: *a Lei Crime Companion Novel (Marcella Scott)*

Unsound: *a Novel (Dr. Caprice Wilson)*

Wired in Paradise: *a Lei Crime Companion Novel (Sophie Ang)*

Middle Grade/Young Adult

Path of Island Fire

Women's Fiction/Romance:

The Waiting Room

Sign up for news of upcoming books at ***http://www.tobyneal.net/***

CPSIA information can be obtained at www.ICGtesting.com
Printed in the USA
LVOW11s0029151014

408811LV00009B/169/P